THE BOOK OF
NONEXISTENT
WORDS

THE BOOK OF NONEXISTENT WORDS

STEFANO MASSINI

Translated from the Italian by Richard Dixon

HarperVia

An Imprint of HarperCollinsPublishers

THE BOOK OF NONEXISTENT WORDS. Copyright © 2018 by Mondadori Libri S.p.A. All rights reserved. Printed in the United States of America. No part of this book may be used or reproduced in any manner whatsoever without written permission except in the case of brief quotations embodied in critical articles and reviews. For information, address HarperCollins Publishers, 195 Broadway, New York, NY 10007.

English translation copyright © 2021 by Richard Dixon.

Illustrations © 2020 Carl Hanser Verlag GmbH & Co. KG, München.

HarperCollins books may be purchased for educational, business, or sales promotional use. For information, please email the Special Markets Department at SPsales@harpercollins.com.

Originally published as *Dizionario inesistente* in Italy in 2018 by Mondadori Libri S.p.A.

FIRST HARPERVIA EDITION PUBLISHED IN 2021

Design adapted by SBI Book Arts, LLC, from the German edition published by Carl Hanser Verlag GmbH & Co. KG

Library of Congress Cataloging-in-Publication Data has been applied for.

ISBN 978-0-06-300478-8

21 22 23 24 25 WOR 10 9 8 7 6 5 4 3 2 1

Contents

THE BOOK OF
NONEXISTENT
WORDS

The Words You Don't Have

I T REALLY ALL BEGAN WITH *ENOUGHNESS*, ALSO called *Morosinitude*. Don't go rushing to the dictionaries— you won't find those words there for the simple reason they don't exist. The same with all the words set out in this book. I've invented them myself. And not out of choice but out of need. Let's take one step back to see why I decided to coin a word after Francesco Morosini, a seventeenth-century Venetian commander.

So, I was going through one of those moments in life—which luckily happen—when some more responsible part of me takes the initiative, makes its voice heard above the jumble of thoughts, and tries to restore order. They are moments of absolute clarity, though sometimes very painful because they upset the system of reflexes and silences that keep me going. It's when a sudden flood of light illuminates the meaning of some of the relentless battles I've been fighting for a long time, hellishly difficult but still deeply necessary, so that my very identity somehow felt tied to them. We'll return to this discussion later, but for the moment, suffice it to say that I was asking myself the crucial question: is it really worth it? And a shiver ran down my spine.

Not only because I was suddenly aware of the complete stupidity of my battle, which I had gradually raised from a paltry guerrilla attack to the status of a crusade. There was no doubt I'd been fooling myself for a long while; the feeling of being on the barricades had filled me with a strange fortifying relish, and yet by drinking that elixir I had avoided asking myself the other real question about the battle: what is it actually all about? Even more disturbing, however—if that were possible—was something less obvious, which I had to explore at all costs. It was like when a detective, even after he has solved his case, glimpses the shadow of a hidden accomplice who had played some key role. So, who had fought against my clarity? Who had added to that enormous waste of energy?

The answer startled me: it was my language. Or rather, that baggage of words we habitually use to describe feelings and states of mind, wrongly thinking that they cover the whole gamut of our emotional universe and that, if anything, it is we who don't know how to use them. But my vocabulary was anything but extraneous to the crime of which I was accusing myself: this was the very reason why I had thrown myself for years into relentless conflict. Just think about it: there's no such word as *enoughness*. There's not a single word that describes the virtue of saying *enough* in the face of pointless battles. On the other hand there are plenty of words that praise the perseverance of the warrior: *constancy, tenacity, determination, obstinacy* . . . Indeed, it seems there's an unwritten rule that deters me from quitting and, to force me to carry on, lacks the words that justify surrender.

It's a fact that language is never neutral; it implies a system of values, and it applies them tyrannically, choosing what to define and what to leave unnamed. Each language, like a piece of clothing made to measure, reproduces what a civilization believes to be right or wrong. Starting with states of mind—indeed, perhaps these above all.

For example, the Utku, a small Inuit population (we'll come across them again later), don't have any name for anger. They fear rage more than anything else and therefore stop it from appearing by not dignifying it with a word. But how many states of mind are not considered in a language, and vice versa, how many are described in curious ways? The Koreans use the noun *han* to indicate a particular gloomy kind of hope, when the prospect of a better future clashes with resigned acceptance of a lousy present. I defy anyone not to have experienced it. And yet we don't have an exact word to express it because our morality (first classical, then Christian) always pitches us into the future, not allowing us any hesitation, as if it were a danger to be warded off. The German language too has a magnificent word, *Torschlußpanik*, to describe the fear of missing crucial moments in our lives as time slips through our hands. Russian then amazes us with such a simple sound, *toska*, to describe a complex state of mind, the sadness that creeps in for no apparent reason and afflicts us until it becomes almost a physical pain. The Japanese word *shoganai* condenses into a single noun the need to carry on without looking back, accepting that everything may have its meaning but doesn't necessarily fall under our control. A remarkable synthesis, I would suggest. It can be bettered only by Indian wisdom, which has a single word—*viraha*—to express the sensation of someone who, at a moment of separation or abandonment, recognizes only then the full strength of their own feeling. I could go on.

And here was where a new state of mind appeared, a mixture of annoyance and surprise that my language was not a palette of colors I could use to paint all things. No indeed. It was some kind of cage in which I didn't want to stay. But then, in the end, aren't words supposed to be tools created to solve problems? There's always an old trick behind every word: we name things in order to be understood; we describe concepts and situations to avoid misunderstandings within our tribe. Because no one ever talks only for themselves: words are a bridge between us and others, built over the river of things. So the point was to restart the wondrous mechanism that has fed our dictionaries from time immemorial. If a word was missing, I would create one. Or at least I would suggest one. But how?

To begin with, a name had to be given to my withdrawal from a pointless conflict. It was then that I thought about the words taken from characters from the past: we have the word *Stakhanovite* because the Russian miner Alexey G. Stakhanov beat all records for dedication to work, digging out several hundred tons of coal in a single shift. In contrast, an *Oblomovist* is someone who can't move from his couch, in homage to that wonderful hero Ilya Ilyich Oblomov in the story by Ivan Goncharov. He sought refuge in the arms of his sofa after having escaped from the relentless suffering of his office. And then, still in the workplace, there's the word *Luddite*, with which we brand anyone who fights against the spread of technology at work. It is said that Ned Ludd was the first English worker to vent his anger against a steam-powered loom. These three words were created from three stories, three portraits, three people: Stakhanov, Oblomov, and Ludd. If we have any doubts about the real origins of the words we use, we can be cheered by these nouns directly derived from specific names: each word hides a story, and its discovery takes us to the root of its meaning. By accepting this method alone, what an infinite catalogue of stories opens up before us!

In the mid-nineteenth century, a popular French novelist invented a successful new saga, published in installments. Pierre Alexis Ponson du Terrail was a slapdash, hack writer, but that didn't prevent him from achieving great fame with the bungled adventures of a cutthroat thief who then has a change of heart. We won't find Terrail's works in bookstores today, yet the French adjective *rocambolesque*, inspired by his character Rocambole, has crept into many languages to describe daring adventures. Similarly, we are constantly, and unknowingly, raising the ghost of King Louis XV's minister of finance, who at the end of the eighteenth century taxed anything suggesting a minimum of wealth, from furnishings to the facades of buildings. France sank into a kind of depression from fiscal vengeance, and the surname of the infamous politician came to indicate everything that is stark, plain, and unadorned. His name was Étienne de Silhouette. Then, during the same period, a certain Philibert Commerson, a respected naturalist, made a journey around the world to catalogue flora and fauna in the Southern Hemisphere. The head of the expedition was the famous navigator Louis Antoine de Bougainville, from whom the plant we all know takes its name. But more curiously, this was not the only species to be baptized on that journey. On his return, Commerson fell madly in love with an attractive woman to whom he dedicated the most beautiful of all flowers, showing her an exotic example collected from the other side of the world. The woman was Hortense Barré, and it was after her that the hortensia, or hydrangea, was named. In the same way, the Duke of Wellington became associated with the famous boot and an unspecified Dame Jeanne gave her name to the glass wine vessel known as the demijohn. Which just goes to show how what we say is often built on stories crystallized over the years into the remnants of a sound.

Irony sometimes has a life of its own, and I'm ready to bet that five centuries ago the valiant nobleman who led the French army would have been most unhappy for his name to be linked to an amusing episode that occurred after his death: within a few years the inscription on his tomb had eroded so that the words IF HE WERE NOT DEAD, HE WOULD STILL BE ENVIED (French: *envie*) could be misread as IF HE WERE NOT DEAD, HE WOULD STILL BE ALIVE (French: *en vie*), hence the noun *lapalissade*, inspired by Jacques de la Palice.

But if this colorful array of heroes had succeeded in being converted into as many words, why couldn't I find inspiration the same way? I could create my own noun, starting with a suitable story. And I thought immediately of Morosini.

In 1645, Francesco Morosini was one of Venice's most dependable hopes: twenty-six years old, a man who shunned danger with that healthy dose of recklessness that makes all the difference in a soldier. But it just so happened that the first war in which he found himself also lasted rather a long time. Indeed, far too long.

Much of the Venetian colony in Crete had fallen into the hands of the Ottomans, who had only to launch the final attack on the capital, Candia. It was expected to be a siege of just a few weeks—the Turks pressing at the walls from outside, the Venetians holding on inside. The troops of Saint Mark were led by the young, enterprising Morosini. And he, it has to be said, knew how to inspire his men. The troops of Ibrahim I and then of Mehmed IV gave no respite to the Venetian stronghold, but no one was prepared to surrender—for twenty-three whole years. Which means that Morosini, who was dark haired when he arrived at Candia, had turned almost gray by the time he left. Yes, he did leave. Because in 1669, after years and years of strenuous resistance, at a cost of almost 140,000 deaths on both sides, Francesco Morosini decided the time had come to utter the crucial word: *enough*. He sought an interview with the sultan and negotiated a dignified exit. After which, tired and exhausted, he sailed home at last, proud not to have gone on any further. What a liberation! What intelligence! To know when to bring the curtain down regardless of the distorted notion of virtue that harries us with the same old words: "Carry on fighting, always, despite everything."

Well, Morosini proved the opposite.

And he didn't just prove it. Henceforth he embodies it some way, because I've decided to name my word after him:

> **Morosinitude** (otherwise called *enoughness*)—*noun.*
> Derived from Francesco Morosini, a seventeenth-century Venetian commander (1619–1694). *Indicates the sublime virtue of someone who, in the face of a pointless battle, has the courage to pull out.*

I already seem to hear the horrified reactions of those who would prefer us to use roundabout expressions rather than flood the holy lexicon with new and arbitrary creations. What I do know is that language—a splendid invention of the human being—is fluid, constantly in motion. We express ourselves as living creatures, and we talk with the specific purpose of making life better. We might say that our need to share is just as important as our need to feed ourselves: we wouldn't be human if we couldn't tell stories. So what's wrong if from each story a word is created? Isn't it, after all, a way of remembering or endorsing the experience of the past with a word of warning for the future? Yes, because the truth is that Stakhanov, Silhouette, La Palice, and all the others have contributed in no small way toward helping the human race, allowing us to better express the complexity of our feelings—even those of the simplest kind.

And since I really do believe that anyone able to find the right words to tell their story is in some way saved, I will never feel guilty about having transformed Morosini into *Morosinitude*.

So those who wish can follow me in this collection of non-existent words. I have chosen them for all those moments of "If only there were a word to express it." One last thing: these inventions of mine will only really acquire a meaning if you add your own, with no qualms or embarrassment. Because language is there not simply to be studied; it is created, changed, adapted, modeled, distorted, expanded, cursed, reembraced. In short: it becomes our own.

Which means living it, now and always.

A

Annonism
and Anchorism

WE ALL SHARE ONE THING: WE ALL DRAW UP our own escape plan. And it goes without saying that some of us actually carry our plan out, while others are happy to spend their whole lives painting the walls of their cells blue and pretending they are clear skies and open seas. But that's fine; there is really very little difference because it's not escaping itself that makes us human but the urge to do so and, with it, the irrepressible need to know that an escape route actually exists.

Our lives, in the end, always have something to do with one fact: we refuse to admit we cannot fly. It's the only real problem we have, to which we are never properly reconciled. Because wings, yes, they would give us the chance to get away, always, anywhere, above all from this accursed force of gravity that keeps us anchored to the ground in every respect. And so Daedalus and Icarus are fine, Leonardo da Vinci's flying machines are fine, whole volumes of mythology are fine, and legends in which angels and gods humiliate mortals with a flap of their wings.

In this craving to possess the sky we have also managed to contradict ourselves, as is demonstrated by those two French brothers Joseph and Jacques Montgolfier. They devoted every moment of their lives to conquering the realm of the birds, but as soon as they created the first craft that could lift people from the ground, they took fright. Everything was ready, planned, and built: the basket attached to a balloon (which they proudly baptized with their surname) was finally there, waiting to take them up, high, higher, where only immortals had been. And yet the two brothers had second thoughts, so the first beings to explore the skyways were a goat, a rooster, and a duck. It was 1783 when this Noah's Ark lifted off before the incredulous eyes of thousands of humans, all of whom stayed firmly on the ground, watching from the houses of Annonay. So this pleasant town in the Ardèche carries the memory of our siege on the sky and, at the same time, our reconciliation with it. Why did the Montgolfier brothers hold back from what they most wanted to do? Was it cowardice? Or an excess of prudence? In either case, there is something of Joseph and Jacques in all of us, torn as we are between our urge to fly and our fear of actually doing so, which throws us off balance. Man tries to explore but at the same time is frightened of exploring. And while the inventions stall, the only adventure is given to a goat, a rooster, and a duck, the aviators of Annonay.

But that's not all. I think there's another underlying element. The earth, though still much unexplored, is nevertheless a well-ordered stockroom in comparison with the sky. That's why, even though we hate our limitations, we prefer to keep firmly attached to them. What attracts us to the boundlessness of space is also what frightens us about it: the total, infinite freedom inside which one can lose oneself and be forgotten.

This is an interesting idea as the subject of a word: the fear of losing oneself or being lost from others, exactly as happens when our eyes inevitably lose sight of a bird as it flies away. But from where—or rather, from whom—do we begin building our word? There's an endless list of possibilities among painters, poets, scientists. You will come across many of these in the following pages. Some of them are household names, thanks to their glorious deeds. And yet it just so happens a relatively unknown American marine, Charlie "Bud" Cowart, comes to our aid. And who knows how he would have felt on a particular morning in 1932 if he had been told that many years later he would have no less than a word named after him.

Who was Charlie? A kid not yet seventeen, though he looked somewhat older. Stocky, well built, even elephantine in the way he walked, always leaning forward, Charlie was living proof of that strange natural mechanism by which boys reach adulthood, that long stage of development in which they generally resemble a gawky gnome and are rather dimwitted too. Despite having enlisted in the United States Navy, the new recruit Cowart seemed more than anything like a stumpy pixie of a seaman. In his chubby cheeks was a vague apathy, as if a mysterious veil separated him from the outside world. Was it some kind of defense? No, not in his case. Quite simply, Charlie always felt like one of those kids who hung about at the door, neither entering nor leaving, and this limbo had become his home. Those around him began to worry: he was padded by such a dense layer of indolence that he no longer seemed to notice anything, nor even to react. Sometimes he even seemed unaware of reality, simply floating along in it, like a body at the mercy of the current. Weakness? I would say uncertainty. After all, he wasn't short on physical strength. Charlie fought in boxing tournaments where he even showed some natural talent. But it seemed he couldn't land his punches outside the boxing ring: everyday life proved too complicated for him to choose his adversary, whereas in boxing he was given one problem at a time and didn't have to justify each punch. And this fine forbearing kid contented himself with life's occasional thrills only when he put his gloves on, while everything flowed around him almost as though it had nothing to do with him. When he wasn't wearing his official uniform, he always went out in the same old jacket, whether it was raining, blowing a gale, or set to be the hottest day of the year. And just as he never changed the way he dressed, the expression on his face was also identical: jovial but distant, innocently disinterested.

It was in this manner that Charlie Cowart arrived with others at Camp Kearny, never for one moment imagining what awaited him on May 11, 1932, one and a half centuries after the first flight of the Montgolfier brothers' balloon at Annonay.

As they approached the base they couldn't fail to see the cheering crowd that lined the road, but what possible excitement could there be in a military zone? The answer came from a four-year-old boy who sat smiling on his father's shoulders. When Charlie stared at him from the truck, as if to ask the reason for the smile that gladdened the boy's existence, the child just looked up at the sky, as if the gates of Valhalla were about to open. Yawning with his usual apathy, Charlie leaned out from the truck's canvas canopy just far enough to see the aircraft above, and . . . Indeed what he saw was no less amazing than Valhalla: a giant airship, USS *Akron*, pride of the US Air Force, was floating low in the sky. A flying beast, 785 feet long, enormous in every way, in whose belly, it was said, were at least five P-26 fighter aircraft ready for attack, so that the *Akron* was known by everyone as the "flying aircraft carrier." The *Akron* was the most recent incarnation of the hot-air balloon, the latest surprising development in our journey to the sky.

This was why the army had summoned the men to Camp Kearny: it needed at least a hundred seamen to moor that innocent-looking airborne pachyderm looming over their heads, like a vast whale with wings.

"Good thing there's not a breath of wind today," someone murmured, immediately silenced by some self-styled authority on the modern air force: much more than wind was needed to make that leviathan tremble.

Maybe. Meanwhile the base was infected by a blend of excitement and alarm. The *Akron* was certainly a marvel of technology, capable of flying nonstop between New Jersey and California, but there were those who hadn't yet forgotten the many zeppelins caught up in all kinds of accidents during the Great War: it was a fragile giant, easily prone to disaster.

In the general bustle, the other recruits were each assigned a task. They were told—with many well-printed illustrations—that the great monster had to be anchored to a series of vast metal rings fixed to the ground. Each man was assigned to a numbered cable: Charlie Cowart's was number 14. It required a perfect team effort to fix all the ropes, a moment after which the main cable—a hand's width thicker—would be attached to the mooring mast. Easily said. Preparations went on for at least an hour, and when everything was arranged, an officer gave the agreed-upon signal. The young sailors feverishly set to work, like ants, drawing the ropes toward the winches and chanting in time as they pulled, so that the landing of the *Akron* would take place slowly and evenly. It was a true spectacle to watch, and several times the crowd of onlookers burst into spontaneous applause.

It's a fact that applause has a language all its own. Like tones of the human voice, it manages to convey endless shades and degrees of meaning. That day, for example, it was clear to everyone when the crowd started to have their doubts; their clapping lost its bright tinge of congratulation and was converted, if anything, into encouragement.

The men needed it.

Because the clear sky had turned milky white, and now the impressive silhouette of the great airship became like a lake of ink on a sheet of paper. But above all, the mooring procedure was complicated by the wind, which arrived all at once, almost as if to join the party, though hardly welcome. The *Akron* was seen to move a couple of times to one side but was brought back into position by the system of ropes amid the thunderous yells of the officers on the ground. "The leash!" the officer in charge shouted through a megaphone. This technical jargon referred to the main cable, the one that would actually hold the tip of the airship to the iron tower fixed to the ground, like a dog on a chain. At least thirty sailors held the end of this rope, attaching it to its ring, high up, on the mooring mast, to the delight of their comrades who were anchoring the smaller trail ropes with increasing difficulty. Charlie Cowart's hands were burning terribly, despite his gloves. And yet he wondered whether his most pressing anxiety was the pain or the realization that the wind was blowing more forcefully, sending at least twenty of the men's hats flying into the air.

Once the leash was fixed, everyone could at least give a smile of relief, almost as though man had tamed the fury of the elements. But the relief was short-lived. A sudden, stronger gust of wind caused many of the recruits to lose hold of the trail ropes, and the airship lifted vertically, like a child's kite, attached only by the main cable. What was going on? The unimaginable: the majestic heir of the Montgolfier brothers was adrift, at the mercy of the air currents. And since it was fixed to the tower, all the water from its ballast bags was pouring to the ground, so that it was becoming lighter and more uncontrollable by the minute, with three or four sailors plummeting to the ground as they let go of their cables. "Cut the leash!" someone shouted, and in the general panic, this was taken to be an order, regardless of who had shouted it. So a sailor rushed forward with an ax and cut the mooring cable, which was what had been preventing the *Akron* from rising still farther. And by this they actually lost it: the airship went out of control. They watched it rise up and flail like a leaf in the wind.

At least two hours passed without anyone managing to do anything. The storm blew, and it was impossible to consider retrieving the ropes and returning the now humiliated *Akron* to its moorings. The crowd meanwhile was slowly dispersing, one by one, as soon as the people realized it was rather unpatriotic to stay there watching the ignominious defeat of a marvel of the US Navy, which had already cost the lives of several young seamen. And so, in the Californian sky over Camp Kearny, there was soon little left to watch. There was silence, a rarefied and futile silence, until sometime later someone took a pair of binoculars and raised his finger to a point beneath the *Akron*, now several thousand feet from the ground.

"Oh God, no, not this . . ." muttered the officer, who had clearly only just realized that something appalling was happening up there. He dropped his binoculars in fright and called for help, announcing in desperation that something terrible was going on around the airship. The others nearby strained their eyes, trying to work out what could be more terrifying than the *Akron* being tossed about by the wind . . . And very soon they realized what it was.

Apprentice seaman Charlie "Bud" Cowart was still, unbelievably, attached to his rope: he had managed to tie it to his waist, and had been flailing about in the air along with the *Akron*, at an indescribable height, going higher and higher, up to two thousand feet, there, where no one had ventured alone. Too small to be seen from the ground by the naked eye, he had been hanging under the airship, on which no one aboard had questioned whether one of the seamen might have been caught in the cables. So Charlie had been left there, for hours, forgotten to the world—no one had asked about him, no one had noticed he was missing, no one had heard his cries from up there, while he was being blown in every direction by the wind. A curious fate: a kid who floated about in reality, never treating it with any serious concern, now found himself floating in the air while the rest of the world had failed to note his disappearance. Charlie experienced for himself, that day, what Joseph and Jacques Montgolfier feared they might have discovered, up in the air: abandonment by the rest of humanity, the loss of a feeling of self, maybe even an extreme experience verging on death, seeing that souls fly into heaven. Such fears are, after all, deeply human, for we are terrestrial creatures, made to live together, searching for our own reflection in the eyes of others. It is therefore natural to be afraid that humanity might forget us, letting our own small identity drift away into an endless space, into a no-man's-land. Of all the stories I have managed to collect, this story about Charlie describes best of all the real value of the word *solitude*. It doesn't mean cutting ourselves off from others but recognizing that we live in a space different from that of others, that we are elsewhere, two thousand feet up, tied to a cable, and no one seems to be aware of it.

From that day on, Cowart's nickname was "The Anchor." How strange, if we think that during those desperate hours when he drifted through the sky, forgotten by the world, that he felt exactly the opposite: unanchored, detached from everything, watching humanity from outside, from up there, from above. And even when he returned to the base, the terrible experience of his flight never left him: we are human only when our feet are firmly on the ground.

Maybe having lost any desire for two wings.

Annonism—*noun.* Derived from the town of Annonay, where the first balloon flight took place, though with no humans aboard (1783). *Indicates the contradiction of* *someone who, having sought in every way to be free from something, abandons the possibility of fully enjoying it out of fear.*

Anchorism—*noun*. Derived from the nickname The Anchor, describing the fate of seaman Charlie "Bud" Cowart (1932). *Indicates the state of mind of those who feel forgotten by the rest of the world, realizing that the life of everyone around them carries on just the same regardless of their own personal suffering.*

B

Biroism
and Bicism

I F WE CATCH SOMEONE STARING AT US WHILE we're walking along the street, it most likely bothers us. Other people's glances are generally unwelcome. We regard them as intrusions; we imagine the person watching is searching for some confirmation of their own superiority. We're so lost in our own galaxy that intercepting signs of life in the universe often seems unimportant, and if we accede to those signs, it is merely through a morbid desire to pat ourselves on the back for the shortcomings of others. It's no wonder, no surprise, then, if the sensation of being watched is the same as that of being judged, being put on trial, examined in our every detail: young people reject the gaze of older people, to whom they immediately seem to ascribe heaven

knows what deviation, just as older people see in others' eyes a certainty of caricature. In short, there's a net prohibition on eye contact between strangers.

And yet observing others can sometimes offer unexpected revelations, if you only accept that each detail overlooked contains a potential lesson.

We have an example of this in the remarkable story of two Hungarian brothers, László and György. We're in the tumultuous 1920s, and while Europe is getting ready to show the worst of itself, the two young men are earning their living with whatever

the streets of Budapest have to offer. László is shy, lanky, and bright-eyed, one you might almost think can see right through you, reading your thoughts like articles in a shop window, until you realize a moment later that the kid is wholly unpredictable. Be prepared for sudden changes, because László possesses unexpected flashes of vitality that sometimes unmask fake introverts.

Among his beer-drinking companions, all this is no surprise. László is known—more than for his long silences—for those sudden caustic barbs that show not only that he is alive and well but also that he is tougher and more acerbic than ever. And they are clever quips that often become legendary among his fellow drinkers, so that our hero has earned the reputation of a wise twenty-year-old, which, if nothing else, is good enough to persuade his fellows in existential crisis to pay his round of drinks: this too is a job in its own way, and in hard times nothing is to be ruled out. It's just a shame that László in conversation, as in everything else, even in the way he dresses and shaves himself, is an incurable daydreamer. Indeed, much more: a fugitive. Because the daydreamer is simply someone who can't pay attention, whereas the fugitive deliberately decides to escape from others. Or perhaps, who knows, to escape even from himself. László is like this. His thoughts fly elsewhere. He is incapable of perching on a branch and building a nest, so he has to flap his wings continually in the air, always fooling himself that the next tree will be the one from which to admire the landscape. And to call it his own.

No one knows all of this: László is brilliant at seeming just distracted. His brother, György, is the only one not to spare him from the truth. Not László or anyone else, since György is razor sharp and hits the bull's-eye with every shot. In this respect, to invite him to your table is quite risky: he'll always manage to figure out what the others are trying to hide, maybe even from themselves, because, as a good chemistry graduate, he has the formula that makes acids react with bases, and by adding salts he can set it all on fire. Result of the experiment? Hardly anyone still talks to György. His brother is the only one who (precisely because of György's scientific malice) considers him a real laugh. People look at them and think: *What a pair—it's hard to find two people more different.*

No one can work out why the brothers have never been seen to argue; nor can they work out how they cope with the highs and lows of such a harum-scarum daily existence. There's no job László and György haven't at least tried, from driver to customs officer, from dealer to journalist, without disdaining even hypnotist and surrealist painter. With the paltry income from this precarious lifestyle, the two of them make ends meet, helping each other out in times of need and toasting the occasional success. Of course, when your pockets are empty and any wage is welcome so long as it can be turned into food, then any future is open to consideration. Especially if you're a Hungarian Jew at the very moment when your country is making eyes at a certain mustachioed Hitler from Berlin who is promising to avenge the unhealed wounds of the Great War. And yet the imminent—and inevitable—storm doesn't seem to frighten the two indomitable brothers: they still put their faith in their own intuition, trying to convert it into ready cash, and meanwhile they don't stint on criticizing those in power, so that László carries on writing articles under his own name for the socialist newspaper, whose rival, the popular *Budapesti Hírlap*, is a mouthpiece for the most rabid Magyar nationalism.

So we can imagine him, one pale morning, sitting at the window of his modest apartment, which hardly exceeds the bounds of dignity, with a half-blackened stove and ugly wallpaper with purple diamonds on a green background. This is a workers' district. An indefinable odor of home cooking and sewerage wafts through the streets while a factory chimney fills everywhere with smoke as soon as the wind rises in the west. Silence is impossible: a bunch of kids amuse themselves playing marbles in puddles right under his window, though the distinction between playing and fighting is hard to draw. While he seeks inspiration for his daily article on the labor rights of mine workers, László loses himself in the byways of thought, and for at least ten minutes he stares at his ink-stained hands. Everything in this house is smeared with ink: the cloth on the only table, the edges of every book, the cuffs of his shirts, even the lapels of his beloved overcoat, consigned to the pawnbrokers several times and luckily always redeemed. But what, after all, is this torrent of ink if not the hallmark of those who earn their living from words? László is proud of it. Or rather: *he was*. Until today. Because the human spirit is like this: what you were proud of until yesterday, all of a sudden you hate. And that is precisely it: through some unconscionable attack of bourgeois snobbery, our journalist for *Előre* is quite unwilling to let his hands become as black as a miner's. Who cares if coal gets into your lungs and the ink from a fountain pen reaches no farther than your fingertips? To make a living from words, do you really have to welter in flecks of pitch, finding fingerprints even on your cheeks? It is said there's a moment when all workers curse the tools of their trade: blacksmiths their anvil, carpenters their plane, midwives their forceps. And so, on this fateful day, László—who had changed profession a hundred times—suddenly feels like an ancient scribe and declares war on the fountain pen that stains his hands, his existence, his clothing, and his house. At this point our hero's spirit of observation now suddenly makes all the difference, for in that peak of anger, László's eyes settle on those kids, on their marbles. He watches a marble roll through a puddle and straight out, leaving a smooth trail of dirty water.

He watches. Observation really is everything. That's what László does that day.

And that marble on a street in Budapest gave him the inspiration for the ballpoint pen. All that was needed was a tiny ball placed on the end of a cartridge filled with ink and it would leave a perfect line as it rolled over the paper. Enough of the fountain pen and its deplorable leaks—a Jewish hack journalist would change the history if not of literature then at least of writing. For such an invention there had to be a special ink, less liquid than that of fountain pens, and ideally faster drying . . . Wasn't his brother, György, a chemist, even if marred by the sourness of a disagreeable character? Thanks to the collaboration between the two brothers, the patent for the ballpoint pen was registered on June 15, 1938.

"What name do you wish to give to your idea?" the clerk behind the desk asked as he cleaned the ink stains from his fingers. "Biro pen," they answered with a smile, since their surname, like that of thousands of other Hungarians, was Bíró. After which, having paid the necessary taxes and duties, they probably went off for a drink. Who, in their place, wouldn't have done the same? The patent for that revolutionary pen could perhaps make them millionaires: a couple of glasses of pálinka was the least they could do to celebrate.

Exactly.

Except that their excitement over the invention might have somewhat distracted them from the general situation, which didn't look good for the Chosen People. During the festival of Shavuot it is said that if children stare into the sky they can see heaven open for a moment in all its splendor. Who knows if the Bíró brothers ever saw it. What is certain is that at the height of the Third Reich, they saw the terrors of hell open, not in the sky but beneath their feet: having registered their patent, they had to listen to the rabbi, who told them to escape. Escape? For a natural fugitive like László it came easily, like telling a fish to get wet. And yet the rabbi wasn't joking—did they really fail to realize? They had to leave, by dawn, before it was too late, with just one suitcase: their most valuable things. And so it was. We can imagine them, the two brothers, laughed at by everyone when the rabbi discovered to his amazement that their luggage was full of prototype pens, bottles of ink of varying thickness, cartridges and tubes of every shape and form. "Didn't I tell you to bring your most valuable possessions?" to which I imagine the Bíró brothers would have nodded, proud of their bags of instruments.

They looked upon their escape as a commercial choice, purely for profit. To make the best of a brilliant idea they had to go as far away as possible, so far away that no führer could ever stain their existence like any old fountain pen.

And they chose Argentina.

Which meant a long, interminable crossing by boat. There, glory awaited. The patent required the journey.

On the day of their arrival, queuing impatiently on deck to be first off the boat, László glanced at his brother, fearing György might read his thoughts. György didn't understand. He smiled and thought the voyage must have tired even his indomitable partner. He hadn't imagined in the slightest that László, there and then, was having terrible, sudden thoughts that came from nowhere: *There's always some trick in store when land appears on the horizon. It always seems as if you can touch it, as if you've already landed, as if you can almost leap off and say the journey's finally over. But it's not like this. The land is playing a trick on you. It's fooling you, laughing, knowing perfectly well that there's still a hell of a lot of water between you and it. It doesn't matter that your destination is approaching, visible—that's entirely irrelevant. What matters, what really matters, is setting foot on the quay, looking back for a moment at the ship, and only then can you say you've landed.*

This, more or less, was what flashed through László Bíró's mind a couple of hours before they said goodbye to the Atlantic. And it's one of those remarkable occasions when—for better or worse—we're suddenly aware of the whole course of events in front of us. It is something sublime and terrifying: our distinction between now and then is canceled, and quite simply we see the meaning of everything, so brightly that it dazzles us. After which, once the brightness has gone, everything goes back to the beginning, the same as before. But only seemingly. Something inside us has changed forever, because it actually knows, has seen, is conscious and aware of, everything. From now on, a strange light in our eyes will say that all was—and is—nevertheless clear.

This is the feeling I have when I look at photographs of László József Bíró, who spent almost half a century in Buenos Aires under the name Ladislao José Biro. Before the camera, he is smiling, always smiling, proudly showing his ballpoint pen, to which he devoted all his energy, even when he was left by himself. But the truth is that László spent the whole of his life as he had that last day on the boat: very close to the port yet far away, close to landing but actually still at sea. The deception of reaching dry land tormented him—he held a brilliant patent, he saw himself a step away from prosperity and peace, but amazingly he never achieved either. The curse of flying without ever perching on any branch made him an unparalleled example of someone whose talent, whose intuition, eluded him. He didn't know how to exploit it. He didn't know how to enjoy it, and the expanse of water between him and the port was impassible. Twelve years after his landing in Argentina, despite all his efforts and investment, the great idea of the Biro pen was still a brilliant stroke of genius with no practical application. Too many mistakes. Too much expenditure. But above all it was the creator himself: something was wrong with his approach; he still had difficulty making ends meet—the same as thirty years before in Budapest.

One morning he received a call from Europe: a wealthy businessman asked him to sell the patent. He would make a success of it, he said; he knew how to do it. He put a strange emphasis on those words "I know how to do it." As if to suggest, subtly, that the chemical formula of success didn't just come through *knowing* but also from *doing*, all in one. And it was as if a seaman standing on the quay were laughing at the boat still at the mercy of the waves, unable to moor. László was tempted to hang up—his whole life was at stake, much more than a simple patent. To give it up for money? It meant declaring once and for all his own eternal state of incapacity, and that would be a terrible admission. He tried to play for time, pretending that his pens were already making him rich. But he was no good at lying, or maybe he chose not to be. His voice began to crack, which didn't go unnoticed. The voice from Europe offered a sum. The other laughed, almost offended. The voice responded with a small increase.

The bargaining, in the end, was not so difficult. They made a deal.

And that was how the ballpoint pen passed from the hands of Señor Biro to those of Baron Marcel Bich (pronounced "Bic"), who transformed it during the 1950s into a worldwide phenomenon. And when László died in 1985, Bich's pens, as the Bible says, increased and multiplied. It matters little that the man who had invented them in Budapest as he watched children playing marbles died in a modest house in Buenos Aires. Among his various jobs, he had worked for many years in the factory of his former supplier.

Which produced ballpoint pens.

> **Biroism**—*noun*. Derived from László József Bíró (1899–1985). *Indicates the state of mind of those who feel very close to achieving what they want and deserve in life. But despite this, they always remain like a ship unable to reach a port.*

> **Bicism**—*noun*. Derived from Baron Marcel Bich (1914–1994). *Indicates the phenomenon of appropriation, not necessarily unlawful, of somebody else's idea for personal gain. In particular, any situation in which the pragmatism of one person surpasses the genius of another who cannot manage his own talent.*

Caransebic

IF YOU DON'T HAVE AN ENEMY, YOU'RE A NOBODY. So much these days seems based on this. The construction of identity comes about through opposition, through negation. It's as though we're incapable of understanding who we are, and have therefore opted for the simpler and immediate question: who are we not? There again, the verb *to affirm* is always complex, implying a responsibility. Whereas *to refute*, as well as being easier, is much more gratifying. We all like to feel we are part of a conflict and needed for some kind of cause that relies on our armed support. So we carry on digging trenches. Our ID cards lack certain details that are crucial for defining a social being, namely information about those we oppose, those against whom we fight, those we brand as our enemies in the great herd of diversity.

But what are our beloved wars really about? They are often

just a chess game against ourselves. We believe we are fighting someone, not realizing that the battlefield in the end is all ours. Ours alone. In the infinite labyrinth of voices that resonate within the human soul, it is so difficult to give a name to every face we have: we are a chorus of contrasting sensations and opinions, between which it is difficult to find harmony. We live by inconsistencies. Indeed, our inconsistencies define us, and are continually hidden and disguised in the name of an absurd command to remain consistent. People cannot be consistent: it goes against their very nature, which fortunately evolves through the shocks of experience. To live is to change, to live is to adapt, to live is to alter oneself, willingly accepting that yesterday's *I* is to be rediscovered in tomorrow's *I*. Every time we look in a mirror, the illusion of recognition leads us to believe that behind a body—always the same—there must live an identical thinking (and sentient) being. Well, that's simply not true: we are not who we were yesterday, for the simple reason that our body replaces between 50 and 100 billion cells a day. At the end of every year, moreover, we have thrown away and renewed a mass of cells equal to our entire body weight. No surprise, then, if the conflict between our own opposing factions continues ceaselessly, against the perpetual odious enticement of inner peace.

It's rather like that famous night at Caransebeş.

It was September 17, 1788, and the umpteenth war was being fought between the Habsburg Empire and its eternal enemy, the Ottoman Turks, in the forests along the border between Hungary and Romania. This time the armies met at the first light of dawn on the muddy banks of the Timiş River. History sometimes chooses the most insignificant places for its set pieces. Wasn't Yorktown—where US independence was decided—an expanse of

barns along a coast that suddenly drops down to the sea? And wasn't Waterloo in the end just an immense flat area battered by wind and rain, between the dark conifers of Charleroi? Not much different, Caransebeş witnessed the clash of arms amid inhospitable woods and villages inhabited by Romanies.

Before recounting the astonishing events of that night, however, I'd like to take you back to the previous year, when it all began.

War broke out in August 1787. And the final day of reckoning would be trumpeted when the sultan's army was at last defeated, demoralized, humiliated, and every other adjective that might describe a foregone victory. An excess of optimism, you will say. Not at all: pure and simple realism, military arithmetic, seeing that the Russian and Austrian empires had recently joined forces. On paper, it was an unbeatable alliance. Just imagine what expectations they had when they lined up for the first battle. We can almost hear the bombastic speeches of the Russian admirals as they marshaled the fleet in the Black Sea. That's right, because this time it was the Russians who started the war—the Austrians would appear onstage in the second act.

All was ready. Flags and standards with the double-headed eagle and Saint George slaying the dragon—slaying the dragon just as they would slay the sultan. Hordes of ships anxious to launch the attack. On the mainland, to enjoy the entertainment, a trio of dancers of the winning side danced the troika, a traditional Russian dance. Except this time it was not danced by the traditional formation of a gentleman and two charming ladies; on the contrary, the tsarina was accompanied by two austere men in full-dress uniforms. Oh, what delightful dance steps! Oh, what merrymaking! As they danced the troika, Tsarina Catherine II smiled, mighty Prince Potemkin smiled with her, and Count

Alexander Suvorov was smiling too, the general of generals, the man reputed to be made not of flesh but of iron, who felt like Saint George with the dragon.

But did they have cause to smile as they danced the troika?

At first it seemed they certainly did: the Turkish fleet was old, in poor repair, worn down by long years of constant warfare. Victories followed one after another, to bolster Russian and Austrian smiles. Dancing the troika was so much fun. Indeed, when all was said and done, this momentous war looked just too easy. Wasn't it a dragon they had to slay? This Sultan Abdul Hamid seemed more like a lizard. A salamander. Just see how the Austrian allies wouldn't even have to enter the field. The Russians would do it all themselves. Should they send the Austrians the lizard's severed head on a tray?

But then news arrived.

Unexpected. Devastating. The poor officer who was given the letter to deliver to Her Imperial Majesty—let us call him Ivan—he trembled with terror, standing immobile at the far end of the room. He didn't have the courage to lift his eyes and see the reaction of these powerful figures. It had fallen to him to deliver the letter only because the men had tossed an accursed coin for it. He kept his eyes down, down, staring at the tips of his boots. He listened to the envelope being opened and the paper unfolded. Ivan then shut his eyes completely. And so, in the crystalline silence, he failed to witness one of those sublime spectacles that have full right to enter Russian history. It should have been a military triumph. A triumph it was, but one of despair. If only Ivan had opened his eyes! He would have enjoyed seeing those smiles slowly disappear from the three faces, corroded into a gnashing of teeth. The oval flesh of rose-cheeked Catherine ever tighter, her jaw ever more clenched. One of the men watching would later swear that he saw Potemkin bite the nail of his little finger, and even iron-spirited Suvorov was showing signs of rust. The first to make a sound was the tsarina: "How can it be that . . ."

And she didn't complete the sentence.

She couldn't. To keep her dignity. Understandably.

I mean, has it ever been known for an imperial fleet to sink, right in the middle of a war, without Sultan Abdul Hamid firing a single shot? Has it ever been known for a Saint George, on the point of slaying the dragon, to die of bronchitis because of too much wind? That night it happened. The storm did everything.

What? The storm?

"Oh yes, Your Highness. Lightning, thunder like never before. And a tempest that shattered the main masts," Ivan explained, just in time to realize that no storm, however legendary, could ever have justified such a disgrace. Because even during the Universal Flood something had remained afloat, for sure, with a certain Noah at the helm. Whereas in this case the Russian fleet had been wiped out, torn apart by the furious waves, and Abdul Hamid was no doubt thanking Allah for his invaluable meteorological contribution.

There: just to remind ourselves under what auspices the war began. But let's return to Caransebeş in September of the following year.

This time the Russians weren't in the game. The satisfaction of thrashing Abdul Hamid once and for all rested in the hands of the Austrian emperor Joseph II, who moreover—we like to think— would have reacted with a mixture of concern and sadistic pleasure at the poor show his ally had put on. Could anyone really lose a fleet in the Black Sea with three gusts of wind? "It would never have happened to us Habsburgs. We enter the fray proudly, all guns blasting, as the Austro-Hungarian army has always boasted. Victory or death. Victory or death. Let them learn from our triumph at Caransebeş."

Exactly. At Caransebeş, on the evening of September 17, there was not a living soul in sight. The first to arrive was a battalion of hussars, who, one might say, were the brave vanguard of His Majesty's Imperial Army. The commander an upright man, hallowed by many years of military service and painstaking care for his authentically Austro-Hungarian mustache—ordered a reconnaissance: to report immediately whether the Turks were already positioned on this or the other side of the river. Yes, sir, victory or death. Victory or death.

After barely an hour, a sigh of relief: no sign of any Ottomans— all silent. Maybe. But the commander, worthy heir of the legendary Count Nádasdy, saw this as no reason for good cheer: Keep watch over the area. Yes, sir. Patrol the banks of the river. Yes, sir. Keep a close watch on the natives. Yes, s—

The natives?

On the banks of the Timiş there were only gypsies.

The commander stroked his bushy mustache: Natives or gypsies, we make no distinction. No laxity allowed. And so it was: Yes, sir, victory or death! Victory or death!

Meanwhile night fell. Ah, what a night it was!

Sweet and terrible. Unforgettable in both respects.

Because it just so happens that the hussars obeyed their commander's orders with a little too much zeal: they patrolled the banks and didn't lose sight of a single gypsy. Except that these *natives* were people with their very own propensity to drink, and when in the company of strangers, they took good care to extend the sacred rites of gypsy hospitality to strangers too. Among such rites were dancing and meats roasted on a spit but above all an alcoholic nectar for which people went literally crazy. And they let it flow. Oh, they certainly let it flow. So that victory and death were quickly forgotten. So that when an infantry battalion turned up, it found the hussars completely drunk, enjoying the feminine beauties of the place. The officers were outraged, and rushed to report the men's shenanigans to their commander. Meanwhile, however, the infantrymen were also tempted by the wondrous liquor, and the party went beyond all moderation. Glasses became bottles, and bottles became barrels. But since a gypsy village doesn't generally entertain whole battalions (nor does it usually invite them to dinner), the disappointment among the soldiers became apparent when word got around that Bacchus had closed the taps: there was a scuffle that turned into a brawl, and from a brawl it was only a short step to gunfire.

When the Habsburg cavalry arrived in all their magnificence, Caransebeş was already in effect a battlefield. Barricades. Smoke. Flames. Fighting everywhere. The battle raged. Austro-Hungarian hussars killed Austro-Hungarian infantrymen in an Austro-Hungarian apocalypse hard to imagine if it hadn't been going on right in front of their eyes. In the pandemonium, amid shouting and gunfire, the hussar commander with the sculpted mustache ran about desperately trying to bring them back to their senses. All in vain. The cavalry had no choice but to throw itself into the fray, shouting, "Halt!" to their compatriots, which was immediately the cause of a further tragic misunderstanding: someone (thanks to the alcohol in his veins) felt sure this "Halt" was an "Allah" and therefore that the cavalry attacking them was none other than an eager Ottoman horde disguised in Habsburg uniforms. Attack! There was more chaos. The Austro-Hungarian army continued fighting savagely throughout the night on the muddy banks of the Timiş, proudly, as it had always boasted. Victory or death. Victory or death. In reality there was more death than victory, since the history books recount that the friendly fire raged for a whole day at least, and even His Imperial Majesty Joseph II was thrown from his horse and ended up in a canal.

Some 9,840 corpses were left on the field. After which, silence fell. Perhaps the most embarrassing silence in the whole of military history.

And it was during this silence, on September 19, that Abdul Hamid's army arrived at Caransebeş, ready to fight. They advanced in close formation, their scimitars drawn and glinting. But the enemy? Wasn't it there? Where was it? They were met by an unexpected calm: flies buzzed everywhere, and the air was thick with a nauseating stench. The banners with the half-moon moved proudly and warlike as far as the banks of the Timiş, and it was there that the grandsons of Osman saw the bloodshed. Some laughed; others felt somewhat disappointed. Once again, as with the Russian fleet, they won the battle without firing a single shot.

Allah is great.

> **Caransebic**—*adjective or noun*. Derived from the Battle of Caransebeş (1788). *Describes the condition of those who, while greatly fearing an external enemy, prevent themselves from fighting it through internal rebellion. The Caransebic can therefore be distinguished from the self-harmer by the simple fact that the former squanders his own energy each time life requires him to confront an external threat, or a so-called enemy. The Caransebic indeed becomes his enemy's accomplice and ally.*

Dottism

I REGRET I'M TOO YOUNG TO HAVE HAD THE chance to meet that genius Dorothy Parker, sometimes known as Dottie. Whenever I am faced with prejudice, I always feel Dottie is needed to destroy it. Her wit was remarkably caustic, capable of dissolving any preconceptions. Perhaps Dottie grew up surrounded by so much dogmatism that life itself had taught her to stand up for herself. Born at the end of the nineteenth century into a Jewish family (by the name of Rothschild), she was brought up by a Protestant stepmother who then packed her off to a Catholic convent. Cruel fate then brought her a rapid series of catastrophes that would have floored even the unbeatable Achilles: her father and stepmother died young, in quick succession, then her beloved uncle, who had adopted her, decided to treat himself to a transatlantic voyage on the *Titanic*. In short, the young girl grew

up with a fierce and irresistible black humor. Death had dogged
her from childhood, and she was keenly aware how important it
was to laugh at it. Always. Which is why she became the most
diabolical scribe in 1930s New York. Her readers knew not only
that Dottie was afraid of nothing and of nobody but also that she
did not fear even her own torments, going as far as to write and
joke about her attempts at suicide. She was ready to shoot at any
target: the fashion for psychoanalysis, her drift into alcoholism,
her disastrous marriages with controlling or bisexual husbands.
It seemed as though Mrs. Parker was invulnerable in the face of

life's calamities and as if the gods of Olympus had ganged up to send her every sort of disaster for the pleasure of seeing whether she would laugh that one off too. One day, in 1938, someone asked her if she was happy: she was rich, respected, powerful, worked in Hollywood, had received an Oscar for screenwriting, and was fought over by the leading US newspapers. So? What did she lack? Dottie was about to launch one of her withering, quick-fire responses. She fixed the journalist in the eye, and said: "A happy woman is always rather less happy than a happy man: I'm that one step short, and it's going to be a pushover."

Exactly: that one step.

Let's go back in time, by precisely a century, to Europe, to track down Henriette d'Angeville, another personality that Dottie would certainly have liked.

It's late summer of 1838. On July 21, Ferdinand II, king of the Two Sicilies, had outlawed dueling between gentlemen. He was unaware that meanwhile, at the foot of Mont Blanc, one of the most pitiless duels of the century was about to begin. This time, however, it was not between two gentlemen but a challenge to the last drop of blood (or rather, the last rock) between a whole community and an amiable noblewoman of remarkable stamina, born forty-four years before in the stately forests of the Jura.

That night in early September, by lantern light, while a steady wind heralded the arrival of fall, a colorful crowd—unusual for that hour—watched preparations for yet another expedition to the summit. Six guides were kissing their wives and children good-bye, warning the more boisterous in the crowd not to upset the horses, nor to set fire to their barns. To one side of the gathering, Comtesse Henriette was sharpening the iron tips of her ice axes with a pumice stone. Something may have distracted her and she grazed her wrist with the stone, causing it to bleed. A young boy in short trousers immediately noticed the redness on her sleeve and hurried across to a well, shouting to everyone: "She's already hurt herself! She's already cut her arm!" They all ran back with their torches, anxious to see whether the "pioneeress" (as the innkeeper at Chamonix insisted on calling her) had sabotaged the expedition before even taking a step. Henriette pretended not to hear. With her teeth she tore a strip of cloth from her checkered skirt, bound it tightly around her wrist, and carried on sharpening the metal, as though nothing had happened. No one had failed to note her expression of pleasure when she sank her teeth into the hem of her dress, and it was clear to everyone that this was a response to the burgomaster, who two days earlier, after a sermon about dignity, had ordered her—on pain of imprisonment—to climb the glacier ("if you really wish to, if you really have to") dressed respectably "in feminine attire." *Feminine attire?* Did he expect her to reach the summit of Mont Blanc wearing a dress?

The burgomaster didn't have the courage to nod. He merely repeated the word *dignity*, loudly and clearly. The comtesse had seriously considered giving the whole thing up, but only for a second. Luckily she remembered the maidservant who years earlier had ventured onto the great mountain as something of a joke and, though carried on the shoulders of men, had reached the summit. That maidservant—a certain Marie—hadn't she also worn a skirt? But it was still to be proved that a descendant of Eve could successfully climb the peak without being held in the arms of an Adam. This was the challenge, and Henriette was ready to meet it. Even in feminine attire.

Among the slate roofs, the bell tower rang out at two o'clock.

A woman from the village—a woodcutter with a pigtail, known for her manly ways—then elbowed her way in among those present, with a pitcher from which she was drinking mouthfuls of milk straight from the cow. Henriette didn't look up; she continued sharpening the seventh of her ten ice axes while the woman used her arm to wipe her mouth, rubbing her lips from her elbow to the back of her plump hand. Then she began her address: "I've no care about you, but have you considered these folk, eh?" indicating the six guides whom the priest was blessing. Henriette neither moved nor showed any sign of offense, so the other woman could do no more than stamp her foot on the ground and click her tongue, as people do when they call a dog, threatening to beat it. The Amazon kept her cool: she was accustomed to scenes like this; she had climbed the highest peaks, from Mont Joly to the Jardin de Talèfre, always defying the prim looks of those who wanted to see women confined to village squares with garlands of flowers in their hair, ready to recite silly poems when their husbands and fathers returned in glory from their expeditions. Well, this time she would be the one to conquer Mont Blanc: she kept repeating it to herself, and who cared that the priest refused to bless her. The great she-bear who was waiting for an answer showed no sign of quitting and stood over her like a hawk over its prey. When Henriette had finished her task and had put the ice axes down among the ropes, she heard the woman's voice again: "I asked you what you'll do if you lose one of them, through this caper of yours. You might have paid them, but it's not as though they're yours. They're not like you, don't you see? They have families . . ."

Another silence. The point of discussion was always the same: in those parts they'd never seen a woman of forty-four who rejected the comfort of the hearth. Just imagine this heretical aging spinster wanting to drag men with family responsibilities to fifteen thousand feet, up among crevasses and ibex, putting even their fertility at risk (according to the doctors, at least, who were sure the expedition would make them sterile). What a shame that the comtesse—rather like our Dottie—was never short of a ready quip: she stared the sturdy woman in the eye, like a rock climber fixing a nail into the rock, and replied, "Better for you: if an avalanche carries us all off, there'll no longer be any guides for a madwoman like me to pay. God protect the mountain from nymphs." And she shouldered her way out to fasten her baggage. The silence had become unbearable, as though it were the last farewell to a procession of men on their way to the gallows. The guides set off along the path while Henriette, beneath her chin, tied the laces of an immense red fur that seemed made almost intentionally to look like the mane of a lion. She grabbed a torch, took a deep breath, and strode out, catching her skirt on a bush. Oh, feminine attire! She yanked the cloth, and with a battle charge she moved ahead of the guides, to her rightful place, to start the expedition.

Comtesse d'Angeville was lucky, at least, that she didn't have to disguise herself or change her name. Some ninety years later—since progress doesn't always produce benefit—Alfonsina Morini had to cut her hair like a man's and drop the last vowel from her first name when she entered the Giro d'Italia as Alfonsin Morini from Castelfranco. There again, what was wrong with a woman wanting to ride in the Giro d'Italia? Alfonsina had every right to race her bike, just as Henriette had every right to climb Mont Blanc.

The fact remained that in the town of Castelfranco, like up there beneath the glacier, it was not every day that a woman pitted herself against men. Especially if her parents were farmworkers and had a lot of children. But Alfonsina was a fanatical cyclist, and always had been, from when she was very young. And she was terror-struck when one night she heard her father, Carletto, ask her mother, Gina: "That crazy daughter of yours—when will she stop pedaling and start bringing home some money?"

Carletto was right. At the age of twelve it was time for a girl to be earning a living. But from cycling, of course—how else? On the other side of the Atlantic, at that same moment, Dottie Parker was also using her wits to make a living, through her talent with a pen. Alfonsina's talent was in her legs and nothing else. There had to be some way of earning money from cycling. And there was.

She turned to religion. Not in the sense that she entered a convent—if it was unacceptable for a woman to ride a bike, it was out of the question for a nun. No, the point was that every Sunday morning she needed an excuse to get out of the house for a few hours, and what better way than to attend Holy Mass? A wickedly genial plan, worthy of Dottie Parker: in the house she fixed a picture of Pope Pius X and would spend a quarter of an hour rattling off prayers each evening before bed. A good socialist like Carletto Morini found it laughable at first; then it occurred to him that it was better to have a pious daughter than a harum-scarum on wheels, and he kept quiet. Alfonsina worked at it diligently and modeled herself on certain holy pictures to acquire a martyred expression of suffering. She spun tales about certain saints, about those who close their eyes, then open them again and everything is full of jasmine. With fancies like that, no one thought it strange for the girl to rush off to church each Sunday. She would leave the house with her veil and dark dress, after which, half a mile from home, she'd take it all off and hide it behind a shrine, useful also for begging the Almighty's forgiveness and at the same time saying: "Lord, bless my legs. Lord, let me win."

That's right, Alfonsina Morini had discovered cycling competitions.

Always on Sunday mornings. "Hi. Is this where you enter the race?" she asked a giant sitting at a table on the first occasion.

"Sure. Just give me the cyclist's name. Are you his sister?"

She shook her head: "Is there any rule that you can't enter if you're a girl?" And since there wasn't, she began to compete.

Okay, fine, there was no money. But the prizes were hams,

bottles of wine, whole wheels of Parmesan cheese. Wasn't this all stuff that could always be resold at market, assuming of course that Carletto had enough to feed the Morini family? What a shame that entering competitions didn't mean winning straightaway. She had to work hard at it, and for some while she didn't place higher than tenth. Then she got better. And better. And better still.

The first time she won anything, it was a crate full of cherries from Vignola. To her they seemed like the most beautiful cherries in the whole of the Po Valley, in the whole world, redder even than the Bolsheviks in Russia. Her triumph, unfortunately, was won with blood—literally, since she crossed the finish line at such a speed that she lost control and crashed into the fountain in the middle of the piazza, cutting her cheek from her ear down. So when she reached the podium she was as red as a cherry—crazy Alfonsina, red Alfonsina.

And it was with this crate of cherries that she arrived back home, still soaked in sweat, with a cut across her face, in her Sunday best, with the pious gaze of Saint Agatha. But there wasn't the usual jollity. All was silent. They sat waiting for her—a tribunal.

"How did you manage to cut your face in church?" Carletto asked, with his hands on the table, sitting among the family members like a government leader with his ministers.

"But she's brought cherries," added the family screwball, Uncle Maso, who was told to have the decency to shut up.

"How did you manage to cut your face in church?" Carletto repeated slowly and clearly. At this point, wasn't it plain to Alfonsina, the pious daughter, that someone must have seen her? No, of all the ways she could have wriggled out of it, she chose the worst: "I banged my head on the tabernacle at San Damaso, and when I reopened my eyes, it was all miraculously full of cherries." And as she said it, she forced herself to cry, as saints do in ecstasy. Dottie Parker would have approved, I'm sure.

But it didn't work. No one moved. Carletto became Signor Morini—a transformation that generally meant the worst was to be expected. He banged his fist on the table as he did at critical moments, and there began a long Lent of abstinence from her bicycle.

But Saint Alfonsina, patron saint of cyclists, didn't lose heart, like Saint Henriette, patron saint of mountaineers, had done a century before. Perseverance is not a female virtue for nothing.

All was perfectly clear—if her father banned her from racing, she had no choice but to find a husband, whoever he was, so long as he allowed his wife to cycle. And she began her search for a consort. Whenever she saw a boy between sixteen and twenty-one, she had just one pickup line, always the same: "Hi, my name's Alfonsina dei Morini. Later you can tell me yours, but do you reckon a wife should be allowed to pedal a bicycle, or not?" One after another, each was crossed off her list. If anyone said yes, that was fine, but then she would add, to avoid any confusion: "My dear, I'm talking about a wife who races, who cycles in competitions, who sweats, spits, flexes her wrists, has swollen veins, grazes her knees, her chin, her hands, who even ends up on a great deep gulch and climbs back out."

Many preferred to change the subject.

Then, just as she was beginning to admit defeat, she found Luigino Strada. It happened at an osteria where, for six lire, Alfonsina washed glasses, wiped tables, and, around closing time, went and fetched the procession of wives who dragged their drunken husbands home. It happened by chance. It happened one evening before the great fair. It happened, and thank goodness it did, because the legs of one who pedals have to keep on pedaling. In any event, the osteria was full. A fog outside in the street and a fug inside, of cigar smoke. Someone broke a glass at a table at the far end, in the corner by the stove: "Alfonsina! Pedal up here, you crazy thing, with a cloth!" because she was the only one of the three waitresses whom they told to pedal. The comment didn't go unnoticed by one of the customers from out of town; "Excuse me, signorina. The bicycle I saw outside on the corner by the church—is it yours by any chance?" Alfonsina didn't even turn to look at him—her father had confiscated her bicycle; she had no wish to explain. But he continued: "If it's yours, I'd like to offer you fifty lire. It's an 1895 Bianchi, one of those with the crest celebrating the twenty-fifth anniversary of the capture of Rome. Excuse me if I ask, but my father was one of the bersaglieri. And I'm also a keen cyclist. My shop, you understand, is on the same road in Milan where Cavalier Bianchi has his factory."

Alfonsina felt a shudder of excitement: "You mean you come from there, the birthplace of the very first bicycles?"

At which the man swathed in smoke replied: "Goodness, it's not as if Bianchi produces bicycles with the help of some midwife! Even if, in all honesty, those cycles are more beautiful than certain children."

Alfonsina Morini gave a start: she was therefore in the presence of a bicycling enthusiast of marriageable age and, moreover, one of His Majesty Cavalier Edoardo Bianchi's subjects. She decided it was time to introduce herself, so she leapt to her feet, slipping on the floor cloth, and ending up literally in his arms, which helped her to get straight to the point. "In Milan, do they let their wives pedal bicycles?" and she awaited his verdict with trepidation.

"Why? Don't they let them here?"

The girl shook her head. "What stupidity," he said. "I'm Luigino Strada, mechanic and engraver. And you?"

"Alfonsina Morini, waitress and cyclist, but more cyclist than waitress. I'm not married, I'm not engaged, I haven't much of a dowry, but in spite of that I invite anyone who wishes to take the necessary steps, within the limits of decency, I mean—I'm not sure I'm making myself clear, Signor Strada. I would like two things, both important. I'd like a husband and I'd like a bicycle."

And Luigino Strada gave her both.

He was always her keenest ally. If it hadn't been for him, Alfonsina would never, but never, have dreamed up the crazy idea of racing in the Giro d'Italia. And yet she went, proud and pugnacious, just like Comtesse d'Angeville on her conquest of the glacier.

What a shame that the two stories share not just the same beginning but, more specifically, the same end.

When Henriette returned to the valley after her conquest of Mont Blanc—and in feminine attire, moreover—there was no party to welcome her back. Instead, a deathly silence. But the worst was yet to come. It is said that when she entered the mountain climber's inn—where she ate venison, polenta, and testosterone in mountain sauce—the chief climber stood up as though he were welcoming a queen, except that he corrected the impression by saying: "Mademoiselle, you think you have conquered the mountain, but today most of all it is the mountain that has lost. Now that a woman has reached the top, mountain climbing will no longer be a delight."

Something similar happened in Genoa at the end of the first leg of the 1924 Giro d'Italia, when it emerged that Signor Alfonsin Morini was in fact Alfonsina, a woman. She was disqualified because her presence brought cycling into disrepute. Into disrepute?

But hadn't she been ranked higher than many others? She was given no chance to defend herself. Then Alfonsina did her own Giro d'Italia, outside the contest, like a circus act, like a puppy in a tutu among clowns.

This, in the end, is the only real difference between Dottie Parker and the two sportswomen: those two didn't have the ready answer that would turn prejudice upside down. Comtesse d'Angeville needed something of Dottie's spirit: she would have replied to the mountaineer with something like "I'll remind you, sir, that the mountain in this part of the world is feminine—*la montagna, le montagne, la montaña*—which gives me rather more right to it than you." And Alfonsina could have done the same. There's always something to learn from women like Dottie: they teach you that the gun should always be kept loaded. Especially if every day a war has to be fought.

> **Dottism**—*noun.* Derived from the nickname of Dorothy Parker (1893–1967). *Indicates the supreme gift of those who are able to transform whatever drama, calamity, or prejudice into a comic interlude. And therefore always into a triumph.*

Related:

> **Henriettude; also, Alfonsinity**—*nouns.* Derived from the mountaineer Comtesse Henriette d'Angeville (1794–1871) and from the cyclist Alfonsina Morini (1891–1959). *Denotes the unequal comparison between men and women, in which the victory of the latter is reduced, debased, and invalidated.*

E

Eastmanian

THERE ARE SOME NOVELS WHOSE IMPACT IS SO subtle that you find you've been hit and sunk without even having seen the torpedo. And then there are others whose power lies instead in a caustic, clear, head-on perfidy. Among this second category I would include, without any shadow of doubt, Jonathan Swift's *Gulliver's Travels*, one of the most merciless books I can think of when it comes to the evergreen question of how human beings compare themselves with others. During his long adventure, the central character's height never changes a single inch, and yet he imagines first that he's a giant (surrounded by tiny Lilliputians) and then a dwarf (with the inhabitants of Brobdingnag over seventy feet tall). How much I identify with this madness of relativity!

The obsession with comparison seems endemic these days, with social media continually offering us models and examples of other people's lives, with an immediate tendency to cast them into higher or lower categories. The feeling of frustration that can arise from this is perfectly understandable on a scientific level. After eons of human evolution, our emotional responses have yet to adapt to life in large cities, where railroad stations are besieged by commuters and you will find yourself from morning to evening shoulder to shoulder with hundreds of unfamiliar fellow citizens. For tens of thousands of years mankind lived in small communities where the social roles were allocated for the single clear purpose of the common good, and therefore each tribe needed only one witch doctor, one crazed prophetess, a larger group of hunters, one military leader, and so forth: there was absolutely no question of holding a contest to decide who to appoint as the holy man, while the chief warrior was decided through combat on equal terms, to be fought before the whole assembled tribe. Again, it was like this for countless years, reducing inferiority complexes and their effects to a minimum. Then humanity got into gear, so to speak, recognizing the numerous advantages of an urban community for mutual defense and an effective sharing of services. It is undeniable: if the village functioned better than the family, the city would multiply those advantages. All quite right. It's just unfortunate that this change has happened so staggeringly quickly while our capacity to adjust is so slow, and no one realized that the concentration of masses of individuals in a limited area would create an inevitable network of comparisons, job rivalry, and a spasmodic tendency to see a chance to compete everywhere. Added to which the whole world, thanks to the internet, was soon to become a single global village, where a New Caledonian businessman could beat his Norwegian counterpart for a building contract. Giants and dwarves, as Swift would say. And when you think that, anatomically speaking, our coccyx still contains the bony remnant of the tail that distinguished our remotest

ancestors, you soon realize what enormous social change has taken place over the past two thousand years. Indeed, we feel defenseless, paralyzed, like the grandchildren of some sorcerer who until the day before yesterday was the only person in the neighborhood to concoct potions but suddenly finds himself hurled into intercontinental competition. Maybe in another two thousand years, when our tails have completely vanished, we may also feel at ease under this bombardment of comparisons. Maybe. Certainly at the moment it's hellishly difficult, and the obsession to compete has become a disease.

Perhaps this is why I feel an urge to reexamine the story of the gangster Monk Eastman and his all-out rivalry with Paul Kelly to win the throne of Manhattan. Let us say that it's reminiscent in some respects of Joseph Conrad's story "The Duel," if it were not for the fact that the bitter conflict between Eastman and Kelly had a heavy cost in human life and brought havoc to the city over many years. But what was to be gained from it? In effect nothing, since the two princes of the New York underworld came from groups that were socially and linguistically quite different, and they could have continued to run their own criminal patches without interfering with each other, whatever the outcome of their personal feud. It was therefore merely a question of supremacy, of who stood taller, Eastman or Kelly.

It's difficult to imagine two more different gangsters. At the time of the war that stained Manhattan with blood, Eastman was not yet thirty while Kelly wasn't even twenty-five—two kids who, instead of making a living behind the counter of a drugstore or unloading crates at the port, found themselves wearing a crown decorated not with rubies but with bullets.

But let's start from the beginning, for it's worth it.

Monk Eastman was one hundred percent Jewish but at the same

time an American, born on the Hudson, son of that tribe of David that landed in the Big Apple in the mid-nineteenth century to seek its fortune. Running through his veins, in fact, was Osterman blood—they were among the most sought-after Ashkenazi cooks in Lower Manhattan—but by the age of twenty he had abandoned his true surname to give himself a free hand, keeping well away from the family kitchen. Not that Daddy Osterman had tried to put a cook's hat on the head of that restless son of his, described by the papers as an overweight chubby-cheeked boar with a permanent grin that turned into a kind of scowl. The real problem was that young Osterman really did resemble a pig. When he was thirteen, some kid in a street brawl called him Porky, and ever since then it remained the ultimate insult, to be used as a weapon by anyone wishing to goad him. It is also said that an errand boy, that same day, was drawn by the yells of the thirteen-year-old huddled against a wall and thought to defend him by shouting that it was a real insult to call him Porky; after which he wiped the blood from Eastman's face and, on looking at him, added that he might at least have been called Monkey. When people talk about central moments in a person's life, well, that was his. It goes without saying that a son branded with the name Porky wasn't exactly an honor for a kosher restaurateur. Eastman left home as soon as he could and took the name Monk, which, in effect, is a shortened form of Monkey. Yes, he chose to acknowledge his animal nature, starting with his name. Don't people say that a kindly face can sometimes be a lifesaver? In Monk's case it was probably his objective ugliness that made him abhorrent. No girl ever accepted his invitation to dance, and even the boys kept well clear of him, knowing their parents didn't like to see them playing with such a zoological specimen. Isolated from human company, Monk therefore decided to look to animals for an appropriate role model. So first, good predator that he was, he chose his territory. He would devote himself to the Bowery, the roughest district and hence ripe for savage antics. It was the last decade of the 1800s, and in the eyes of twenty-year-old Eastman, the great New York crime racket seemed like a newfound gold mine, ready to be exploited. The district offered the delicious potential of gambling houses, brothels, and robberies of every kind, if only someone would actually decide to take control. That was what Monk did, counting on the terror derived from an assured animal fame. And since, of all the species classified by Linnaeus, the human being is the most opportunistic of beasts, it took only a few years before he found himself surrounded by all those Jewish kids who had once insulted him—monkey Eastman may also have been a swine, but in his Bowery pigpen they were making heaps of money. How easily the wind can change direction. Anyone remembering the kid with the unfortunate face found it hard to believe he now ran an all-Jewish gang that may well have abstained from shooting during the Shabbat but laid down the law between the river and Broadway for the rest of the week. The gang eventually counted a thousand soldiers: *baruch HaShem*! Dazzling was the entrepreneurial vein of the new generations—indeed, the very latest generation, since Eastman's lieutenant, his right-hand man known for being the most blood-thirsty hothead of the Jewish gang, was a lanky sixteen-year-old by the name of Max Zweifach, with the bluest eyes in the district: he became a criminal legend for having stuck a fork into the back of a teacher's hand, an episode that marked the end of his schooling but, at the same time, the beginning of his glittering criminal career.

It was just a shame that someone else had an eye on the rich pickings the area had to offer. There were Irishmen for sure, red haired and bloodied because they were formidable knife fighters: their first gang was created simply as a gang of vandals, but over time the Dead Rabbits (remaining among animals) came to be respected by everyone, running the Bowery racket under the protection of obliging cops. Yet Eastman wasn't bothered. The Rabbits had recently become particularly involved in politics, putting their paws on certain public contracts that the Jewish gang had no intention of getting hold of. If there was an Irish threat that disturbed Monk's sleep, it was the Whyos, undisputed bosses of at least twenty saloons near the Hudson. There wasn't much room for negotiation since their capacity for dialogue was fairly limited. Attempting an approach wasn't even in the cards—one word slightly out of place was enough for their colonels to move from the language of words to that of the blade. So it was no surprise when one of their most dreaded henchmen, a certain Pike (yes, the animal lexicon in the gangster world extended as far as fish), was arrested and a list of prices for his services was found on him, which ranged from emasculation to severed ears and in extreme cases went as far as throat slitting. Well, I guess it was this ritual that made Eastman pause to reflect. So he and his men were happy to allow the Irishmen to keep control of their saloons near the river, taking care not to create any mutual tension. By doing so, however, the Jewish expansion focused on the opposite end of the district, namely that five-road junction where the acme of corruption gathered among smoke, prostitutes, and gambling tables. The plan was upset by just one detail: it was an area coveted by another up-and-coming boss, a certain Paolo Antonio Vaccarelli, who hid his southern Italian roots under the name Paul Kelly. While Monk had been branded by Mother Nature with a fat and swollen face, Kelly was the matchless embodiment of Latin charm. Handsome, a master of refinement, and a keen theatergoer, he, at the same time, made no secret about his long ambition to be a boxer, and in this he loved climbing into the ring with the nickname Goldsmith, though he would never, but never, have cast a single gram of gold. But on his olive skin—so Mediterranean—he loved to display a glint of gold chains, rings, and bracelets that made him look like the figure of a saint in procession. So the bestial violence that had elected Eastman as the leader of his men manifested in Kelly as a reverential, even religious, fear, Kelly well knowing that the Lord Almighty might be capable of infinite mercies, such as striking down the people of Egypt. Apart from this difference in methods, during the same time that it took Monk to create his Hebrew gang, Kelly was assembling his own ferocious circle, all Italians. If there had been a greater age difference between the two, who knows whether that crazy contest for supremacy might have been avoided. The fact remains that for years the kings of crime had no higher purpose in life than futile confrontation, ending always in a draw. It would have been comic if the consequences hadn't been so terrible. When the last of the florists dared to say he feared one of them more than the other, that was enough for him to have his shop burned down. Eastman and Kelly kept a constant eye on each other. If one was seen in the company of ten men, the other would immediately appear on the street with fifteen. For years their houses were in the same neighborhood, less than a block apart, so they could keep an eye on each other in an endless rivalry—from what they wore to what food went into their pantries. They competed over cooks, waiters, bookkeepers, many of whom ended up dead as soon as they made their choice. The barber they both went to was subjected to heavy cross-questioning and was threatened many times with the direst consequences if he dared to show himself more partial in any way to the other. Countless prostitutes were disfigured for having extolled the sexual vigor of the Jew or the Italian. On September 17, 1903, this obsession turned into war. For a whole day Rivington Street became a battleground between the sons of Abraham and the devotees of Saint Anthony, and by evening many corpses were strewn across the street. Had it, at least, served to produce a winner? No, not at all. There was a net draw between the numbers of Jewish and Italian casualties. The situation had become intolerable. It was now those same politicians corrupted by the two sides who ordered them to resolve the dispute. Sure, but how? The answer was surprising. Monk and Kelly would sort it out, at last, in the way they had always yearned to. They would fight each other in a boxing ring, in an old storehouse in the Bronx.

And so the unimaginable happened. Two of the most powerful gangsters of all time climbed bare-chested into the ring, wearing boxing gloves, each to prove he was right. According to those present, the match lasted over two hours. Paul Kelly gave the best fight of his boxing career but was unable to hold back the animal fury of a pig with the snout of a monkey. Late into the night, when the two collapsed in exhaustion, a silence fell on that squalid joint, which for one evening had become the true heart of New York.

"Which of them has won?" a timid spectator asked the referee. And he too could only shake his head. Even in the ring, bruised and exhausted, Monk and Kelly had ended in a draw.

Eastmanian—*adjective.* Derived from the gangster Edward Osterman, alias Monk Eastman (1875–1920). *Indicates the obsessive frenzy of someone who ties his whole existence to a constant, devastating feud with others, finding in every fellow creature merely the pretext for a comparison with himself.*

Related:

Gulliverism—*noun.* Derived from the central character in Jonathan Swift's novel (1726). *Indicates the state of mind of someone who fluctuates in self-esteem, continually seeing himself as either a giant or a dwarf.*

Faradian

THE LONG TABLE HAD BEEN LAID, RESPLENDENT beneath the magnificent crystal chandelier. Young Michael couldn't drag his eyes from that mesmerizing dance of carafes and goblets moving between the delicate fingers of the ladies and the pure white cuffs of the gentleman scientists. Someone remarked how 1813 had been a terribly rainy year. And one of the wives immediately turned to her husband as if to an oracle, asking whether all that rain might not portend some vast tidal wave. There were quiet laughs, enough to hide the general embarrassment about such crass stupidity. After which, throughout the entire meal, each academic's favorite subject was the glorious merit of his own research.

It was perhaps the first time that Michael had been properly invited to such a sumptuous feast, in which the enjoyment of the food seemed the last concern, far less than the display of each attendee's credentials. For half an hour at least, the boy observed with a mixture of amusement and disappointment this uncharted aspect of the scientific community, and it seemed so unusual to watch these eminent luminaries, armed with forks and spoons, flaunting their academic achievements like a grocer at an inn might praise the salting of his cod. For Michael, it was a magnificent

spectacle, and depressing too—the great marshals of science were not, after all, so unlike ordinary men, and outside the lecture halls where they teased apart matter, they turned out to be just the same as the grubby-fingered customers who crowded his father's forge. Indeed the baseness of some remarks seemed even lower, if that were possible, than the pearls of certain drunken gatherings he had happened to witness. What a discovery! Meanwhile, amid the clinking of cutlery, the trays of game were served onto plates, and at times it really seemed as if the ultimate reflection of science around that table had to be sought in the surgical skill with which his fellow guests boned their pheasant and rabbit.

Lost in thought, Michael heard the voice of his host asking whether perhaps the meal was not to his taste.

And it was then that he realized he hadn't touched his food, being a thousand times more anxious not to miss one fragment of that improbably anatomical theater. He had to keep reminding himself that he too was now part of this elite circle and had absolutely no need to feel extraneous in any way, especially to the ritual of dissecting the game. Though he came from a poor background and his father was a mere master of the anvil, Michael had gradually earned respect and esteem over the past few years. He had gained not a single notion of chemistry or physics without paying a heavy price, paying at least triple that of the scions of noble birth. And so? What did he still need to fear, now that he was assistant to one of the most celebrated brains of the royal sciences?

And yet Michael still felt he had to ask permission, he who had found his way into the rooms of the academy not as a student but as an errand boy working for a bookseller in Blandford Street. He glanced across to Professor Davy at the head of the table, who caught his eye and may not have known what Michael was thinking but smiled all the same. For Michael it was like hearing him say: "Whatever you do, I'm the one who brought you to this table—you're my right-hand man."

And only then did Michael taste the meat, finding it much less tasty than what was served in taverns.

It was all thanks to Professor Humphry Davy that somebody in the temple of research had taken notice of Michael, his remarkable memory, his remarkable capacity for calculation, but above all that relentless curiosity with which he avidly devoured all the books Mr. Riebau used to send him off to deliver. At the age of sixteen Michael had a thorough knowledge of at least ten textbooks on applied science and was fully able to demonstrate theorems, resolve equations, develop physical propositions. All of this without buying a single volume, just delivering them to people's homes. In the early days there were those who treated him as a circus freak. The youngest researchers had fun testing him, well knowing that this scrawny kid with his pants rolled up at the hems, as skinny as a rake and wearing shoes laced with string, was no competition for them. Where could anyone like him go? Sure, he could describe Otto von Guericke's electrostatic globe better than they could, and he quoted Gray's studies from memory, so that someone secretly went to him, to the errand boy, to get him to correct their paper on Benjamin Franklin. No doubt about it—he was good. Perhaps clever, gifted. But even if he were a new Copernicus, the sciences were not a playground for the son of a blacksmith. He needed a protector, and nobody protects anyone whose shoes are laced with string. For his part, Michael was well aware of this. Intelligence is a nasty creature—you can't just apply it as you wish; you have to deal with it all the time, even when it forces you to understand what you'd prefer never to understand. And he understood—understood everything, like in a trigonometry exercise in which the sum of two angles is measurable without approximation.

Luckily, however, there's an element of chance in life that makes all the difference between human beings and theorems. And this unexpected unknown element determined that one dull rainy day

Mr. Riebau's errand boy should end up delivering a score to the house of William Dance, London's most famous musician.

While the illustrious customer was searching for a few pennies to give him as a tip, a flash of lightning filled the room. Michael ran to the window, counting aloud to the old man's amazement so that he dared not interrupt until the boy explained that the thunder follows the lightning by so many seconds according to the distance at which it fell. "Oh yes? That's good to know. And who told you?" asked Dance.

"I read about it, sir. And anyway, it's a pure physical deduction. If we knew the speed of light, it could be calculated with mathematical accuracy. I'll explain it, if you wish. Do you?"

And since William Dance was a man of natural curiosity, he was very happy to listen for a full two hours to the generous lesson in physics given in his drawing room by the bookseller's errand boy. Surprising. Accustomed to unearthing the talent of young violinists or opera singers, Dance was immediately dazzled by the boy's attunement to science. But how could he remunerate him? He felt the only adequate means of payment was to let the boy have his tickets for the public lectures of one of Britain's scientific luminaries, Professor Davy. The new series would start in a few days' time. The new pupil could not appear in those patched trousers, of course. Dance would pay for him to have a decent set of clothes.

And so, from the following Thursday, there was more than one look of surprise when the bookseller's errand boy from Southwark was seen entering the golden doorway of the Royal Institution and taking his seat in the second row, among the heirs of the noblest families. And who then had given him that fine suit? Had he perhaps stolen it? Or maybe it had been passed down to him?

All of this gossip passed over Michael's head without him being aware in the slightest: his whole interest was in Davy's lectures, which he followed for the entire year, not missing a single one, and transcribing them to the last syllable, so that ten months later he timidly presented the professor with more than three hundred pages ready for publication.

The great scientist hadn't failed to notice the constant presence of the boy in the second row, and the tireless manner in which he followed his every example. But he had never for one moment imagined a work so well done. This was the beginning of a close and lively collaboration, greeted by the whole scientific community with scorn due to the plebeian background of that interloper, always branded as the errand boy. Davy was often asked whether he had considered other candidates before choosing someone whose wardrobe might still contain that pair of shoes laced with string. The professor always defended him, especially when his eyesight was impaired by an accident during a chemical experiment, requiring him to depend even further on his worthy assistant.

These, then, were the circumstances through which Michael came to sit at that feast on the banks of Lake Geneva in 1814. He was accompanying Professor Davy on a scientific tour of universities, taking part in the highest gatherings that Europe had to offer, including social gatherings. A great satisfaction, you might say, an unimaginable achievement for the son of an ironworker. I agree.

But storytelling, first of all, involves choosing a story line—where you wish to end, or, in other words, on what detail you want to drop the curtain so as to leave the listener happy or sad.

The story I have chosen, for example, might easily be presented to you as an idyllic friendship between a great academic and a humble errand boy, ending here to everyone's satisfaction. Except that the picture would be incomplete. To tell the full story, we have to introduce Professor Davy's dreadful wife—known also as Widow Apreece—one of the most odious portraits of a woman I have ever encountered.

She was also there at that famous dinner.

Indeed, what is more, had she not been there, then probably no one today, more than two centuries later, would have known anything about what took place at that gathering in Geneva. So let us see what happened.

As young Michael was enjoying his plate of game, proud to find himself welcome among the pupils of Aristotle, it just so happened that one of the fellow guests had the unfortunate idea of railing against the poor quality of his metal fork, which had bent and snapped in the breast of duck. Mrs. Davy, a London socialite of exquisite beauty, previously married to one of the world's wealthiest men, the late Shuckburgh Ashby Apreece, remained unperturbed and, without looking up from the meat still on her plate, addressed Michael with a tone of voice that everyone could hear: "You're the expert on metal, if I'm not mistaken . . . Explain to the professor."

"Have you conducted research on iron?" the rector of the local university immediately asked.

"Not him, his father," she replied, sipping her wine and dabbing her lips with her napkin.

"At which laboratory?" the oldest guest asked with much interest.

Michael was paralyzed, unable to say a word. But it would have been a hundred times better if he had managed to do so, for the tongue can be more diplomatic than the eyes, and the look he gave Widow Apreece was an eloquent declaration of scorn. The young man quickly realized he was a novice in circumstances such as these—no one in the world would ever have risked challenging her, the most dreaded and most practiced in social demolition. Michael had studied dozens of books on the empirical sciences, but as for the science of society, he was still a schoolboy. And he was inevitably humiliated. Widow Apreece's face opened into a radiant smile, almost as if she expected nothing else. She made a hurried gesture to Michael with her right hand and pointed to the kitchen door, adding with a fake yawn: "I've finished eating, Mickey. Take my plate away."

There was a moment of puzzled silence.

The widow smiled to everyone as if to suggest that the scene was perfectly ordinary, then turned to Michael and clicked her fingers at him. How could Mrs. Davy treat her husband's assistant like a servant?

Because she could.

Jane Apreece had never approved of her husband's decision to promote the errand boy and on their departure from London had made it clear to both of them. So far as she was concerned, whatever he might be now, that boy would remain a servant no matter what. Moreover, their faithful valet had been unable to accompany them on the journey, therefore leaving the place vacant for the blacksmith's son. It all made sense.

Professor Davy, for his part, had pleaded with her in every way, praising Michael's scientific achievements and the vast admiration he was beginning to enjoy in academic circles. All in vain. For Widow Apreece, the young man could be a chemist's servant or a physicist's servant or, if he really wanted, an academic's servant, but always in the realm of servitude. Whether he liked it or not, she would always treat him like that.

And since for some undeniable reason wealthy wives—especially pretty ones—are able to manipulate men's firmest wishes in whatever way they please, transforming them into acquiescence, Michael found no help this time in the professor's gaze. He had to get up from his seat, dutifully take the widow's plate, and leave the room to join the cooks in the kitchen.

This was what happened throughout the journey: he was forced to travel on top of the carriage and sleep in the servants' quarters in hotels. More than once, if he was complimented for his scientific contributions, Michael heard himself immediately summoned by the widow for the most menial tasks—to look for her fan or dust down her traveling coat. It is said that in the presence of Alessandro Volta the viper even threw him two coins as a tip. It didn't bother her in the slightest that meanwhile, as each day passed, Michael Faraday was becoming recognized as one of history's most important physicists, outdoing even the fame of Professor Davy himself.

And many years later, when he was a fellow of the Royal Society, even then, on seeing him from her carriage in a London street, Jane Apreece stared at him, clicked her fingers, and threw several pennies on the ground. Faraday was honored by Queen Victoria and lived in lodgings at royal expense at Hampton Court, with a butler and servants.

But to her he was still an errand boy, promoted to valet.

Faradian—*adjective.* Derived from the physicist Michael Faraday (1791–1867). *Indicates the state of mind of one who, in spite of all effort and talent, still feels disparaged and underestimated in another's eyes. Because in life, whatever you do, there is still someone who insists on treating you like a valet.*

G

Gamainic
and Grantairic

LET'S SET OFF ON A SHORT VOYAGE AROUND friendship. It's not easy to talk about: everything has already been said about it and repeated, starting indeed with Aristotle, according to whom the absence of friends is an almost certain guarantee of unhappiness in life. But the philosopher wrote quite a lot more in his reflections on friendship, such as how important it was that there should be no hidden practical motives behind a relationship: the *useful* friendship—as he put it—would always be tainted in comparison with one that seeks only good, or pure and simple sharing. Nothing to argue about so far, you might say.

But Aristotle then went on to add something about differences of origin and points of view. True friendship—according to him—is based on fellow feeling, on a shared approach to life, thinking along the same lines, and he therefore invited us not to rely on strange attractions between those of very different character and background. Ah, a note of discord. Can we only be friends with our equals? Hollywood would have much to say about that, since friendship between opposites offers fertile ground in many a hit movie. Or is it merely a commercial invention? This, indeed, is what I'd like to consider here—friendships that we might call unequal. Was the great Aristotle right, or have the last 2,300 years proved him wrong?

In an imaginary trial, he would certainly take the part of the prosecutor and in his argument would no doubt cite François Gamain. How could anyone disagree? Indeed, this story seems bound to disappoint the most fervent disciples of the goddess Friendship. Judge for yourself. François was the son of Nicolas Gamain, a master locksmith who knew the strengths and weaknesses of every door and drawer in the palace of Versailles. His son had naturally followed in his father's footsteps, specializing in strongboxes and reinforced cupboards, which moreover fits perfectly with our reflection on friendship. How often has it been said that a true friend is one we can trust with our most intimate secrets, knowing that they'll never be betrayed? Well, François was a true master of his trade, one who earned his living making chests that were impregnable.

Now, the interesting part of the story is that toward the end of the eighteenth century our humble craftsman became a friend of none other than His Royal Highness King Louis XVI. A king and a locksmith, both about the same age—one of the oddest couples that history has handed down to us. Yet it is rather less surprising if we consider what a strange character the king was: a true model of inconsistency. For Louis XVI has always been depicted

as the glory of the ancien régime, an epitome of lace and ringlets, and this is absolutely true. But it is equally true, surprisingly, that he'd always had a passion for handicrafts. He carved wood, ground metal, engraved materials with the enthusiasm of an apprentice, and who cares if his guardians considered it rather unbecoming. I find it hard to picture a king at Versailles wearing work gloves beneath his puffed sleeves. And yet it's true—Louis XVI adored his workshop; it was his passion. And it seems he was quite a good craftsman, with a particular talent for metalwork. Who had taught him? François Gamain. To me, it's a touching image, of a king who spends many hours with his friend among vises, cutters, and anvils, to the embarrassment of his bewigged counselors, who on being asked, "Where is His Majesty?" would answer with the most fanciful excuses: "He's gone to the library to study the situation in the colonies . . ." Anything to avoid saying that the king of France was downstairs madly playing at being a metalsmith. It was a close friendship between Louis and François. And how could it not be, if we think that the young locksmith was the only person not flattering the king in the hope of receiving a ministry or an embassy? As they soldered or worked at the lathe, the two thirty-year-olds each learned something from the other, and the king even admitted his own secret anxieties. The crucible was boiling around him, and the fury of the people was about to explode like a stream of incandescent metal. So one evening, as the situation was deteriorating, His Royal Highness made a request to his friend. He had to construct the strongest safe ever made. Walled into the core of the Tuileries Palace, a few steps from the king's private study, it would keep France's secrets, those on which the entire fate of the realm depended. Gamain didn't even need to say yes. He picked up his tools straightaway to show that in a few days the safe would be ready.

And so it was.

But in the meantime the king's fears were proved more than justified. The royal family was placed under guard by the revolutionaries, and the road to the guillotine now seemed certain. During the dramatic month of November 1792 the king was interrogated and there was argument over whether he should be put on trial for attempting to escape. And yet something about his accusers' arguments puzzled him: they gave him the impression they were holding the winning card and were ready to use it when the right moment came. It was clear they knew something. But what? King Louis thought of all his closest advisors, wracked his brain during sleepless nights trying to work out who could have betrayed him, perhaps to save their own life. He could never have imagined that it was his friend the locksmith who had gone to the Revolutionary Committee and handed over the keys to a legendary safe hidden in the Tuileries . . .

I know, you'll say it was all to be expected, to Aristotle's delight. The king and the humble locksmith were too different, too far apart to be true friends and allies. And yet if we thumb through the pages of great literature, the great Aristotle would seem to end up in the minority after all. Let's take a look at the list.

Virgil invented the story of Euryalus and Nisus, who were of different age and military experience. Euryalus is described as a young boy with no more than a few hairs on his cheeks, whereas Nisus is a champion greatly admired by everyone, a true lion in battle. And yet, Virgil writes, the two were inseparable, so that they would die together during a night raid on the camp of the Rutili, like two US marines against the Vietcong. Touching. Nothing like François Gamain.

Just the same story from Ludovico Ariosto, who, in *Orlando*

Furioso, presents a scene with Cloridan and Medoro, both Saracens but one is a sturdy warrior and the other is fair skinned and as blond as a cherub. Here too the friends look death in the face, and Medoro happily risks his life in the vain attempt to rescue his everlasting friend. Doubly touching, for here is a Virgil in multiethnic hue.

Victor Hugo is even more daring in *Les Miserables*, in which he portrays the revolutionary band of students ready to climb onto the Paris barricades in 1832. The leader of the rebels is one Enjolras, whom I've always imagined to be someone so thoroughly restless that he can never sit still. Enjolras is a born instigator, one who doesn't even need to have arguments to convince you because it's more than enough to catch the glint in his eye—a defender of some ancient sense of justice. But while everyone is swept along by his innate passion, only the cynical Grantaire seems immune to the contagion. Members of their group see Grantaire as an intruder, and he is sometimes so cold as to irritate his listeners. It's always the same with any political association: there's usually somebody who expresses their militancy in the form of a cosmic skepticism, almost challenging the very status of humanity as a rational species. This is why I have always been struck by Victor Hugo's perspicacity in placing Enjolras's passion beside Grantaire's disastrous phlegm: the two are opposite poles in political activism, which depends, until proved otherwise, on the extent to which a population believes in justice, on how it responds when called to action, and therefore what prospect there is of awakening, of informing, of stirring it. Of directing it. Rarely do we find two figures so far apart in political debate—Enjolras represents each of us in our strongest and most fervent convictions, represents our urge to act, to take part in the fight, to make a contribution knowing we are crucial and necessary, whereas Grantaire expresses the submissive side that tells us in some way to give up, to lift anchor and sail off, leaving the others (or perhaps no one) to do something in our place. At different times we are all like Enjolras and all like Grantaire. On June 5, 1832, in Rue de la Chanvrerie, while the rebellion is raging on the barricades, the two young men are both present, though each in the conspicuous absence of the other—Enjolras is fighting against the soldiers of Louis Philippe, while Grantaire is holding faith with his cynical disillusionment by dozing off, drunk, inside a famous inn called the Corinthe. After all, isn't this what happens each day on our own barricades? Are we not determined and warrior-like at first, before then plunging into despair? And this truth is what makes the ending all the more vivid when the rebels are defeated by the National Guard and the revolt turns into a manhunt inside Corinthe. Enjolras is alone at this point. They have all escaped or died; he is the last to resist and the last to proclaim his ideals. His gun is jammed, his jacket torn, and yet he still has the strength of will to offer himself to those who want him dead, shouting like a Homeric hero: "Shoot me!" And there beside him, at the last possible moment, Grantaire suddenly appears. He could run off, save himself. No one would see him; he is no more than a harmless drunkard with not a single mark of blood to raise suspicion. Yes, Grantaire could get away.

But he doesn't. He joins his friend, the one so different from him in every way, the one he has hated and yet admired despite their contrasting points of view. It is he, Grantaire, who takes his hand. He fixes his eyes on the soldiers and shouts: "I'm one of them. . . . Finish both of us at one blow." And so it is that the two fall together, hand in hand, feeling they have never, in the end, been separated.

Around the same time, in Italy, a poet called Giacomo Leopardi was launching his own attacks on the fleeting illusion of friendship, which, in his view, was an impossible sentiment among hordes of dismal opportunists. Maybe. And yet life often holds unexpected surprises.

In 1830, Leopardi was able to escape from the awful suffocating imprisonment of his home in Recanati and could breathe once more in the streets of Florence. Here he renewed acquaintance with his Neapolitan friend Antonio Ranieri, whom he had met two years before. It's hard to imagine two more different young men: Giacomo and Antonio. One a poet, the other a dandy. One sickly, the other sturdy. One a despondent thirty-two-year-old, the other a daredevil twenty-four-year-old. One hopeless with women, the other a Casanova in great demand. Plenty here to appall any Aristotle. And yet against all expectation, the two struck up a memorable friendship. It all stemmed from Leopardi's terror of having to go back home. Recanati was Alcatraz—he was terrified at the mere thought of returning. Nevertheless, the genius had no money. His finances would allow him just one final long-yearned-for moment of respite before the precipice. Do you know what it's like when your last path of torment seems set? With Leopardi's Calvary certain, Ranieri appeared on the scene. The handsome young man with his typical Neapolitan fatalism made a grand gesture (though in reality he lived on loans) and invited Leopardi to stay with him on the slopes of Mount Vesuvius, whose beneficial qualities were well known. Hurrah for Ranieri, hurrah for Naples. What followed was a coexistence of opposite spirits, each remarkably tolerant of the other. Leopardi forgave Ranieri for all he loathed about blustering humanity; he even overlooked the comings and goings from his friend's bedsheets of Fanny Targioni Tozzetti, whom Giacomo himself adored. At times it seems as though concealed in such an unlikely friendship was the poet's envy for a world palpitating with urges and passions that had always been denied to him and yet which Ranieri so well embodied. Being his guest in Naples enabled him sometimes to forget how the Church had banned the publication of his *Operette Morali*, but much more important was the help and support of that shrewd and enterprising young man, one of life's buccaneers, whom Leopardi looked upon with tremulous respect. Exactly. For who among us hasn't felt like something of a Leopardi? In friendships we sometimes seek affection from a part of us that we don't understand, that we fear, or simply that we don't have the courage to explore. And I think Antonio Ranieri—whom Leopardi called Totonno—was the Leopardi that Leopardi didn't know; he was Giacomo's repressed self, the hidden and unexplored part of Giacomo, the part of himself he therefore loathed. In his friend he loved his intimate enemy, and whether Aristotle would have liked it or not, this was enough to cement a true friendship. Because friendship in the end is a mirror, the clearest and most reliable mirror in which we can work out who we really are. That's what happened there. Or was it the case that Giacomo—while he lived in the shadow of Ranieri—was able to connect with areas deep down inside him? It's enough for you to know that he was seen filling his eyes with the chaos of the fish markets, playing auctioneer at the lottery, daring to walk out at night among down-and-outs, even gorging himself on pastries, creams, cakes, and candies of every kind until he was sick. Thanks to his friend's influence, Leopardi betrayed Leopardi by acknowledging his other self. Whether he was sitting at the cafè in Largo della Carità guzzling sorbets or scoffing his daily pastries at Pintauro's in Via Toledo,

Leopardi was searching in food for the living matter, the substance, for which he felt a disgust and, at the same time, a craving. Master and slave of his exceptional intellect, he finally recognized another magnet of his being, in his stomach, and in such a way that, while killing an organism already suffering from diabetes, he was at last listening to a silent voice in his internal monologue.

Yet much the same happened to Ranieri, if we accept what he wrote about the bizarre friendship of those years. Totonno himself became something of a Leopardi, softening his excesses, since in every friendship the osmosis is always reciprocal, and Euryalus discovers the Nisus he doesn't know was there.

Meanwhile the poet's state of health deteriorated by the day. Antonio and his sister Paulina became his scribes and his nurses, practically throwing out the promiscuous maidservant who considered the hunchback Leopardi to be a spreader of tuberculosis. By June 14, 1837, Naples was already rife with cholera, and Leopardi's sickly health required him to breathe the purer air of Torre del Greco. All was made ready for his departure, but the carriage never left Vico del Pero in the Santa Teresa degli Scalzi district. The previous day had been Ranieri's name day, the feast of Saint Anthony of Padua, and he had celebrated as he did every year with bagfuls of delicious confetti from Sulmona, sugar-coated almonds. Leopardi had eaten over three pounds of them, plus a chocolate drink and a lemon granita. Within a few hours, the sickness destabilized his already weak health, causing him to collapse, so that by nine in the evening, dying in his friend's arms, he uttered his last words: "Totonno, I can't see the light anymore," and though there was no firing squad, it was rather like Enjolras and Grantaire holding each other's hands at the very edge of the abyss. It is even said that Ranieri, to save his friend's corpse from the ignominy of a common grave, staged a complex diversion with a funeral for an empty coffin. A legend. But it was he, most certainly, who soon erected a monument to his memory as well as took personal charge of publishing all his works.

However it might be interpreted, it was the end of a great friendship and had been a wondrous meeting of opposites—not so dissimilar to that between two other young men, Franz and Yitzchak, in 1911.

It was a wet autumn evening in Prague when young Franz Kafka saw the Polish actor Yitzchak Lowy onstage in a run-down Jewish theater. They were about the same age. One was lanky and bright-eyed with sharp cheekbones and angular gestures, like a satyr from a bygone era, though charged with electric current.

It's impossible to say whether Lowy was a good actor: the animal frenzy in his performance certainly couldn't leave anyone indifferent, his commendable determination touching even the coldest hearts. And more. Let us say the boy put everything into what he did: his feverish movement on the worm-eaten planks of the stage was much more than a job; it strayed into the shameless assertion of a right to declare himself alive. As for Kafka, seated in the stalls with his briefcase on his knee, buttoned to the neck in his overcoat for fear of draughts, he looked up at him like a schoolboy to his teacher, or like a Leopardi to a Ranieri. Here too, it need hardly be said that these two were opposites in character: Franz was an unsettled employee in the insurance business, a visionary with a divine talent who was still unable to find his own direction in life; Yitzchak, on the other hand, had followed his passion for the theater, turning it into a job against all odds and wise advice. These were the competing forces: Kafka the repressed challenged Lowy the fugitive. Kafka, who would have liked to live by his pen, admired in Lowy what he had never had: his force of mind, his control over his own direction, the sacrosanct power to say a clear yes or no at the crucial moment when everything can change. In short, Kafka submitted to himself, whereas Lowy didn't: Lowy managed to transform passive floating into something that resembled swimming. Victor Hugo's two heroes constantly reappear with different names throughout the course of history. Who knows whether Lowy, for his part, saw in that painfully shy young man the flash of genius that he himself would have liked to possess. He probably did, since we are unresolved creatures, and it is only friendship that makes us complete. For Lowy, Kafka was the very personification of art, the absolute and invigorating reason for its expression and for its creation: that boy did not perform other people's ideas but produced them himself through his own inexhaustible and fertile imagination, so that the two complemented each other in a perfect and reciprocal way. And so, on that evening, among the moldering and ramshackle wings of the Savoy, a friendship was born that would change them both forever, which goes to show how we are always looking for someone who challenges our own set ways for the sake of diversity, just the same as gales of wind help trees to rid themselves of dead branches. Young Kafka, the son of an awkward and overbearing father, found friendship as a means to break free, so that he could finally put his name on the deed of a life hitherto on lease. But since the path of every life follows a set of rules all of its own, it is curious how Kafka's followed a different route from that of Leopardi's. While Giacomo sought his partial emancipation through food, Franz decided to emphasize his difference from his father by becoming vegetarian (writing with a certain touch of pride that his father covered his eyes with the newspaper so as not to see his son's plate piled with dates, citrus fruits, and raisins). And while the union between Leopardi and Ranieri continued until the very end, the bond between Kafka and Lowy was unbreakable as well, though maintained by letter. It is said that the only time Yitzchak refused to go onstage was the evening in 1924 when he received news of his friend's death, and a part of him died forever. Once again, Enjolras and Grantaire faced the abyss hand in hand.

> **Gamainic**—*adjective*. Derived from the locksmith François Gamain (1751–1795). *Describes any pact of affection, friendship, or collaboration destined to be broken through the excessive and unbridgeable distance between the parties. With a more extensive and cynical connotation, the adjective warns of the supposed fragility of all relationships between opposites, however idyllic they may appear: "I've seen them together, but to me it all seems too Gamainic."*

Antonym:

> **Grantairic; also, Totonnoic; also, Lowyan**—*adjectives*. Derived from the character of Grantaire in *Les Miserables* by Victor Hugo (1862), or from Antonio Ranieri, nicknamed Totonno (1806–1888), or from Yitzchak Lowy (1887–1942). *Describes any pact of affection, friendship, or collaboration determined by the deep strength of the relationship, overcoming the most radical differences between the parties. In a wider context, the adjective indicates the unfailing strength of a relationship between opposites, destined to withstand every test. And to disappoint Aristotle.*

H

Hearstian

I N THE MID-SIXTEENTH CENTURY, THE COLEGIO
de San Gregorio in Valladolid, Spain, held what was pur-
ported to be a debate among theologians. In reality, however,
the subject of discussion was very specific, and would have consequences for the global economy. It was to consider whether the
Indians of the New World could properly be regarded as creatures
of God, made in his likeness and image, or whether their status
wasn't to be found among animals. In other words: did the Indigenous peoples of the Americas have a soul?

Naturally the question had far-reaching implications: human
beings could not be treated as slaves and gaily subjected to torture,
rape, or death. On the other hand, no criticism could be leveled
against the Spaniards or Portuguese if it emerged that the descen-
dants of the Incas and the Aztecs were more akin to the monkey

than to *Homo sapiens*. And perhaps it was due to the delicacy of what was at stake that, after a year of scholarly disquisition, the congress of Valladolid ended in a stalemate—the parties agreed there were good arguments on both sides, and it was impossible to reach a final verdict.

I have always thought this impasse at the Colegio de San Gregorio to be a rather interesting example of the typical embarrassment that frequently paralyzes us each time we realize that our declarations of ideals compel us to acknowledge certain practical consequences. Thoughts, as we know, remain closed up in that

private movie theater that is our skull, whose seats are all reserved for its owner. But as soon as our thoughts are translated into words, then everything assumes a social significance. Every word we speak is always something that affects those around us, and as Sigmund Freud observed, there's not a single syllable that doesn't have an emotive effect. Words are incantations that move others to laughter or tears, that annoy them or cheer them. Words are a commitment, which ought to be put into practice.

At least in theory.

Because the perverse law of self-interest often introduces a crucial interval between our extravagant words and the actual will to carry them out.

This is what we will now attempt to consider: our own personal Valladolid debate, promptly ended with a suspension of judgment, because the truth is that we are all hostages, forced into the hollow gap between our assertions and their practical implementation.

The story I would like to tell you is that of the publishing magnate William Randolph Hearst, known as the inspiration behind Orson Welles's masterpiece *Citizen Kane*. Hearst was a man obsessed with making money, to the extent that we might picture him modeled on the mythological portrait of King Midas: everything that Hearst touched seemed to turn to gold. His father, George Hearst, had already performed miracles during the California gold rush from which he had built an empire. But if the legend of Midas ends with the much-envied Goldfinger, haunted by his obsession for gold, begging the gods to take away his gift, for William Randolph Hearst there is no trace of such a conversion: for years he kept omnivorously and insatiably expanding his wealth, flaunting it in shameless luxury. His residence was a palace more than a home: the castle housed saccharine reconstructions of Roman temples and pools as far as the eye could see, as well as a zoo with dozens of examples of African species. And it was in this West Coast Versailles, one fine day in spring 1941, that His Majesty the Sun King watched a private screening of Welles's movie. The bosses of RKO, the producers of the movie, had sent him a copy and were concerned about how the most powerful American publisher was going to react. Closed inside his personal movie theater, sitting in religious silence on a single reclining seat in the middle of the room, Hearst let the scenes run through to the very last frame. An anxious bevy of assistants waited in the next room for the outcome.

When the door opened and Midas appeared in cheerful good humor, many heaved a sigh of relief. All he could say was: "Fix a coffee at RKO tomorrow morning." And without betraying the slightest hint of irritation, the world's richest man vanished into the garden, following a pair of new peacocks that had been brightening the lawns for the past three days.

The next morning, wearing the whitest suit in his wardrobe, Hearst warmly greeted the president of RKO, refusing his invitation to sit on the large corner sofa. He remained standing at the window, dramatically backlit against the morning sun in an effect that Orson Welles would have much enjoyed. And in the calmest of ways he began by asking: "How long have we known each other, George?"

"For years, William," the president proudly and affably replied, happy to be party to this affectionate exchange of first names.

"And two people who've known each other for years, George, know a thing or two about each other, do they not?"

"Of course, William, much more than a thing or two."

"So you know very well who I am. You know my father had a gold mine, you know I'm in love with a showgirl, you know I run newspapers and radio stations, that I collect artworks and live in a castle. All these things you know, George." And he smiled with a mixture of narcissism and coolness, displaying his whole rich range of colors like a proud peacock. The president of RKO could only agree, but he felt a sudden dry burning sensation in his throat.

Hearst meanwhile took in one large single breath of air—this had always been his way of preparing his troops for the final attack.

"You asked me to look at the work of that young kid. What's his name?"

"Orson Welles," the president murmured, overlooking the description of "young kid," which didn't augur well.

"You asked me to watch the movie, George, without telling me why. You asked me and that's all. In the note you sent with it you wrote that I might even see some resemblance. That's what you wrote, word for word. Well, I've seen it. And you know what? It's a movie about a guy whose father had a gold mine; the guy falls in love with a showgirl, runs newspapers and radio stations, collects artworks, and lives in a castle. Now I ask you, George: if I get you to watch a movie about a president of a production company who's going bald and wears thick glasses, is the son of European Jews, and has a passion for horses, do you think you might even see some resemblance? Or would you tell me the movie was simply a story about you?"

The atmosphere in the room had become fairly unmanageable, forcing the host to undo the top button of his shirt, under his tie. He tried to reply but didn't have time because an envelope full of banknotes fell on the table in front of him. The contrast of the sun behind Hearst's back had become dazzling: he seemed like a statue of Baal standing on who knows what altar waiting for the daily sacrifice. The god opened his lips to explain: "Here's eight hundred thousand dollars: that'll cover you for loss of earnings and the embarrassment of making that young kid cry. He'll throw a fit like a frustrated artist, then he'll forget all about it. You yourself can burn all the negatives, without telling too many about it. You're the producer, after all; it's yours. Have a good day, George."

He smiled again and moved to the door like an actor at the

end of the last act, ready to return a moment later to thunderous applause.

That bundle of banknotes William Randolph Hearst threw down before RKO's George Schaefer was one of the most remarkable examples of an affront to free artistic expression, as well as an attempt—which fortunately failed—to sabotage a masterpiece. Schaefer returned the eight hundred thousand dollars to its sender, but Welles's movie was subjected to a massive boycott by the powerful networks of the Hearst group: Hearst had simply decided to wipe out its whole existence, denying it as one might do, not with the view of a dissident but with the determination of a heretic. That was his aim, and he pursued it with barefaced efficiency, unhesitatingly. Does it surprise us? No, sir. He displayed the very same attitude, used from time immemorial, that marks the tyrant—a word that originally indicates one who exerts power swiftly and violently. I emphasize: swiftly. It is this aspect that we often ignore in despots: the relationship with time, regarded as a tiresome obstacle to the clear exercise of rightful authority. The tyrant has his very own loathing of time; he detests calm agreement just as much as harmony between his own actions and the space necessary to consider them: there is in him a pathological swiftness, a desperate urge to achieve the result. And since words always conceal an ancient truth, I believe it is truer than ever that power, at its despotic level, is not only violence; it is also (and perhaps above all) swiftness in deciding, immediacy in carrying out, rapidity in declaring that the breeding ground of dissent has been extinguished. Well, on that bright morning at the RKO studio in 1941, Emperor Hearst was tyrannical in all respects. This at least insofar as what he did. But what about his words? Was there a Valladolid debate in William Randolph Hearst too?

Incredibly there was. Because just seven years earlier, in Europe, Welles's future enemy had been present at a press conference given by Adolf Hitler, at the end of which the führer approached him. He knew Hearst's great importance in American publishing and went straight (swiftly, one might say) to the point that interested him: "Why are my politics viewed so badly by you in the United States?"

Hearst glared at Hitler like a teacher might glare at an inattentive schoolchild and gave him a fine lesson on the value of democracy, on respecting press freedom, and generally on America's deep commitment to the right of dissent. The other accredited journalists listened with admiration to that god of freedom as he humiliated the German despot at the very moment when Berlin was crushing every idea that was out of line with the regime. Hearst's words were described as enlightened and illuminating in the dark times of Nazi Germany. This man embodied the clear conscience of one who tolerates criticism and seeks to resolve conflict only through debate. Well done, Hearst, the great Hearst.

Who knows what Hitler would have said if he had seen Hearst offering eight hundred thousand dollars to destroy the movie directed by a twenty-five-year-old. Maybe he would have agreed with his no-nonsense approach, with his firm action. So who really was William Hearst? Should we picture the liberal Hearst who humiliated Hitler or the Hitlerian Heart who brushed away Orson Welles? Before reaching any judgment, it's worth returning once more to Valladolid, to those theologians gathered in the arcades of the Colegio de San Gregorio to tear one another apart for almost a year without reaching a verdict, because there's a clear discrepancy between our words and their consequences, and likewise there's a vast gulf between the Hearst who condemned Hitler and the Hearst who ought to have tolerated *Citizen Kane*. But he couldn't do it, couldn't manage it; it was too much to expect. And I don't know whether Hearst was tempted to apply the same measure for Welles that he had adopted for Hitler. What I believe is that, during the projection of the movie, he had the feeling we all have when we are walking along the precipice of our impulsiveness, and the intoxication of dizziness urges us to give vent to our bodily feelings rather than hold up airy notions. But, goodness, how dreadful to recognize how vacuous our convictions are. To feel we're about to betray ourselves, and that this time—yet again—our only adversaries have just the same face. I fear that deep down there's a Hearst concealed in each one of us, lurking in the barbarous contradictions that bring us into conflict with those beliefs we hold so proudly. Planet Earth is not a place for theories, or for literary salons: confrontation with reality is strewn with jagged glass, and it is rare to emerge from it unscathed. This imbalance constantly sees us as victims and executioners, compelled to recognize the appalling inadequacy of our struggles, deluded into imagining we can put the chaos of our instincts in order. We do not match up to our ideals. And at every moment, in the middle ground between believing and doing, there are heaps of carcasses, tons of wreckage. With the regret of endless missed opportunities.

Hearstian—*adjective, noun.* Derived from William Randolph Hearst (1863–1951). *Describes the contradictory behavior of someone who finds himself acting in a way that is totally opposed to his principles, values, and firmest opinions. As a noun, the Hearstian is someone who cannot reconcile his ideas with his actions, splitting into an uncontrollable dual personality.*

I

Innesian

THIS IS A SIMPLE STORY, PERHAPS THE SIMPLEST in the whole of our dictionary. Once upon a time there was a painter who couldn't paint.

And that's it.

In truth, James Dickson Innes would probably have been a remarkable artist if only he'd had the chance to carry on expressing himself. It is said that painters generally reach their maturity over the passage of time, when their inspiration has the opportunity to match their adult vision of the world and human experience. Well, James didn't manage to reach that stage because a steadfast rival stopped him beforehand, canceling all memory of him. And indeed, I reckon very few of you will have heard of him. The dense mist of time has easily smothered him, to the delight of his opponent.

Sure, the past is full of bitter conflicts. And there's generally only one person who comes out as the winner, even if his methods are sometimes questionable. In the late 1600s, for example, the scientific community was perfectly familiar with Robert Hooke, one of the foremost minds of his age, a most generous inventor and a man with many interests, who could turn his attention to astrophysics, physiology, mechanics, or anything else with outstanding results. Hooke had an undisputable talent for the sciences: he was one of those who ought to be classed as a scientist regardless of whether he actually pursued that profession in life. Yes, paradoxically he would still have been a scientist even if he hadn't made his living on the proceeds of science, for the simple fact that his mind was structured since birth to dismantle reality in the name of numbers. Likewise, Mozart would have been a musician at heart even if he had practiced as a lawyer, because he saw the world in musical terms. And, in truth, our James Dickson Innes would still have been a painter even if he had never seen a canvas: his eyes perceived things in the form of lines, contrasts, colors, so that he painted even without a brush.

But let's return to Hooke.

He was one of the most naturally scientific minds in Britain, yet this didn't prevent his star from setting very soon. Why? Lack of determination? Not at all—on the contrary, his list of contributions to modern physics is unusually lengthy. And so? Was he stopped by gambling debts or a weakness for the other sex? Not that either. Hooke devoted himself to his studies with nothing short of religious zeal. No, his descent into oblivion forever—till now, more than three centuries later—was marked by the fact that he, like Innes, had an enemy. In his case, it was a very powerful one who answered to the name of Isaac Newton.

Seven years younger than Hooke, Newton was—one might say—rather sensitive about competition. Thin, hollowed to the bone by the woodworm of hysteria, the famous physicist was legendary for the quarrels and hostilities he fostered throughout his life, sometimes even trying to filch other men's research to publish as his own. Touchy and quick-tempered, this terrible character didn't go unnoticed even among members of the British parliament, where he sat for several years without ever deigning to speak, except when, in fury, he had it officially recorded that the Palace of Westminster was too cold and its draughts should be fixed once and for all. A truly hateful being. To such an extent that someone questioned where such anger might have originated and suggested it was due to the discharge of toxic substances during experiments. In other words, a kind of chemical monster, one who was so violently abusive that it was quite shocking when he took leave of his senses. The philosopher John Locke had been subjected to such behavior, though Newton had always claimed Locke was a friend. Exactly. Just imagine what he could unleash upon his enemies.

Robert Hooke, on the contrary, was not bellicose by nature: he spoke quietly, often in a murmur, blushed easily, and nodded in agreement if he was ever criticized, rather like those individuals who spend their lives tiptoeing about, always apologizing to humanity for being a nuisance. We have all met someone like Hooke and know how such people are delicate creatures, extremely fragile, so that even the occasional company of a man like Newton—worse still, his hostility—can have devastating consequences.

Despite being such opposites, Newton and Hooke were the two leading British scientists of the late seventeenth century. Newton had earned respect throughout Europe with his studies on universal gravitation, but Hooke's light also shone brightly, for he was the first person to coin the term *cell* and to formulate the law of elasticity. Well, it was this coexistence on the Olympus of science that disturbed Newton's peevish mood and his sleep. He was, moreover, a man universally known for the perilous instability of his nerves. He made no secret of his wholehearted abhorrence of Hooke, a legitimate feeling while kept private, but which clouded his vision, causing him to go as far as physical threats. And it didn't stop there. Newton harried each member of the Royal Society, one by one, turning them against Hooke and discrediting Hooke's years of research. We might have seen Newton, the king of His Majesty's physicists, as he lashed out, purple faced, against the first attendant who dared to mention his rival, with his bewigged colleagues trying in vain to comfort him: "You're mistaken, Isaac. The boy didn't say 'Hooke,' he said 'Brooke'! I heard 'Brooke.' We all heard 'Brooke' . . . And anyway, never mind, Isaac. We'll fire him all the same. Don't cry. Calm down, Isaac. Really, that's it. Take a deep breath. His name will never be mentioned again. Never again."

That's right, never again.

"Robert, my dear fellow, do you think you might reduce your visits to the Royal Society? You know how it is—there are problems with Newton, who might take it badly if he sees you there. You understand—you're more considerate, unlike him. We're asking you to protect the good name of the Royal Society too. What will people think if they get to hear about these wars? Yesterday he was shouting like a maniac. He attacked the librarian when he said that Hooke came before Newton . . . in alphabetical order! It took four men to hold him back. He had his hands at his throat. Can we really allow such scenes? He's a sick man, you know. The mercury vapors are clouding his brain.

It all depends on you, Robert. Don't let yourself be seen, and all will be for the best. We feel sure you understand. You won't let us down, will you?"

For his part, Hooke agreed, as always. Almost seventy, and in poor health, he didn't have the strength to resist, and he cut himself off in his rooms, leaving a sad note: "After death the void awaits me." And it really was like this: the eighteenth century began with Newton's triumphal appointment as president of the Royal Society, while Hooke ended his days in complete oblivion. He died after being told that portraits of him had been removed from the society's corridors by order of the president himself, which is why no one today can be quite sure what the man who discovered the cell actually looked like.

This is enough to explain what effect an enemy can have on the glory of someone who gave his all. You spend years on research, ruin your eyesight reading books, fuse your brain to prove a formula, and for what purpose? For nothing, if there's someone like Newton against you.

The same for young James Dickson Innes. Or rather, for him it was much worse. Hooke had had Newton against him. James's enemy was an inseparable part of himself, so inseparable that it didn't even offer him the satisfaction of telling it to go to hell. Yes, it was his own body that prevented him from painting as he wished. This is his story: about how our sensibility, our will, our talent, can sometimes be mortified and reduced to nothing by this machinery of skin, flesh, bones, and its assortment of liquids. The body can decide to go wrong, not to play its part, not to cooperate. For James it was always like that: he didn't feel comfortable inside that casing of his. He was a skinny, pale boy; it seemed almost an insult to send him outside on cold winter days. And from his earliest childhood he realized his body would be his enemy. None of us remember what our very first thoughts were, having just stuck our noses out into the world. But James was always certain that, on his first appearance among living beings, it was one of disgust. From then on, decisions would be made for him by two lungs, a liver, a gut, and the red-sodden heart muscle that pumps blood from the brain to the tip of the toes, night and day, without being asked. It happened in an instant. James felt taken hostage, like a dog on a chain. Would he always be a prisoner of this bile, this spleen, this stomach, these abscesses, these swellings, this sweat, these broken teeth? That was how it was. No way out.

And the more he discovered his true vocation in painting, the more his body told him it would never keep silent, never allow him to create any more colored bodies on canvas without taking account of his own biological container. There are some lives in which the body agrees to keep quiet, allowing a person to talk, and there are other lives in which the body expects to talk all the time, deafening the room.

The battle between Innes and his very own Newton began in early childhood. From the age of ten he was wracked by fevers, sickness, fainting. This, I think, was why everyone at the Slade School of Fine Art at the end of the nineteenth century was astonished by those paintings of his, so strange and different. What was it about this artist, not yet twenty, that made him so different from his contemporaries? One thing more than anything else: Innes didn't paint bodies. In his pictures there was almost never any trace of a face, hands, legs; Planet Earth appeared as a magnificent deserted wasteland, where no anatomical cage compelled pure beings to come to terms, each day, at every moment, with their organic matter. Humiliated by his unreliable body, Innes imagined a world in which there were no bodies, in which an eternal sense of beauty was expressed only in those austere mountains of his Welsh homeland.

To everyone, he became the painter of peaks, of valleys, of ridges. If there were figures depicting young girls, they were silhouetted against mountain backgrounds so that they too imitated the austere vertical geometry of the landscape. Innes adored nothing more than the purity of those blustery, cold, inhospitable summits, where no fragile body such as his could ever venture. And this did not trouble him; on the contrary: he loved his mountains because of their very resistance to attack, because they could escape the depredation of arrogant humanity. Innes's canvases are therefore a sum of rocks, cliffs, waterfalls, and when he became friendly with the painter Augustus John and spent hours at the easel with him, the contrast became even more apparent: joyous crowds populated Augustus's creations as if they had all jumped out of Innes's landscapes.

Meanwhile his body gave him no peace. He was diagnosed with tuberculosis when he was just twenty-three, forcing him to find relief in warmer climates, such as Spain or Morocco. He endured this constriction like a true exile: an Isaac Newton more ruthless than ever separated him from his beloved Welsh landscapes, not caring a damn about his style, about his urgency, about his need to give his own meaning to life on this earth. Who was he now? A true painter? Or was he just the slave of a rebellious body, a servant who unbeknown to his master found pleasure in painting?

Innes, like Hooke, never really resisted the attacks of his opponent. He tolerated them, overly so, with an irksome resignation. He let his years pass like a squatting tenant, feeling continually exposed to the insults of those who have a rightful claim to the room. He suffered every kind of abuse from the rotten casing that never gave him a moment's peace, which he always regarded as something different and distant from himself.

His was not his own body: he inhabited it; nothing more. He closed his eyes for the last time in 1914, at the age of twenty-seven.

The enemy had won the challenge. And that was that.

Innesian—*adjective.* Derived from the painter James Dickson Innes (1887–1914). *Indicates a feeling of desperate dependence on one's own body, on its physiological demands, on its transformations over time, with the result that it soaks up all one's energy and profoundly influences one's existence.*

Related:

Hookism—*noun.* Derived from the scientist Robert Hooke (1635–1703). *Describes the state of mind of one who is subjected to coarse and aggressive competition, orchestrated by an opponent who is convinced he has to be the unquestionable winner.*

L

Liarism

PEOPLE LIKE TO SAY THAT ANIMALS ARE SPON-
taneous and sincere, naturally lacking in that markedly
human tendency to be false. Well, sadly it isn't true: animals are very good deceivers, especially when they feel threatened.
A clever defense mechanism that scientists call *thanatosis* is adopted by many kinds of reptiles, amphibians, birds, and mam-
mals. Thanatosis is pure theater: as soon as the prey finds itself
being chased, it stops running and shows every sign of being
dead. The limbs contract until they become rigid, the mouth
drops open, the tongue hangs to one side, and sometimes—as in
the case of the opossum—from a special gland it even secretes
the stink of a putrefying corpse. This detail amazes me—I never
imagined the opossum had anything to teach us when it came
to deception. A snake in the Southern Hemisphere completes

the picture with self-induced bleeding to look like a hemorrhage, though many insects can also do this. In short, playacting isn't just a human strategy but a cunning instrument devised by Mother Nature to confuse the enemy. You may remember the story in Greek mythology about Achilles dressing as a girl to avoid going off to war: it was his mother who sent him in disguise to the court of Lycomedes, where the bold youth in his wig and short skirt was welcomed in the royal harem. In actuality, cross-dressing isn't unique to the human race: even plants use it, happy to deceive pollinating insects with a faithful reproduction of female genitalia. There's even an African orchid that is particularly skilled at imitation, capable of attracting swarms of insects with the unmistakable smell of rotting flesh.

This serves to put the subject of deception in a wider perspective, and away from the realm of moral judgment. Humans, like opossums and orchids, playact in order to survive, especially if they feel themselves under threat.

One of the most remarkable examples of these necessary masquerades was Operation Fortitude during World War II. To confuse the Nazis before the Normandy landings, a whole theatrical diversion was set up, called FUSAG, an acronym for First United States Army Group. It was an enormous sham with dummy tanks (inflatable or made of papier-mâché) and battalions of puppets. And seeing that FUSAG was a brilliant success, arousing fear of an imminent invasion from Norway or an attack on Calais, someone even thought of continuing this useful experiment after D-Day, creating the largest military sideshow ever known. In this case the smokescreen effect was created with an army of what seemed like substantial proportions: a meager thousand participants were multiplied out of all proportion with the help of audio effects and

stage tricks. It was decided to create something the size of an epic movie, along the same lines as FUSAG, relying entirely on psychological effect: large loudspeakers placed around the troops broadcasted the recorded sound of ten times the number of armored tanks, along with an equivalent amount of radio transmissions, specially made to be intercepted by the Reich. Theater techniques were used to fabricate at least one whole military camp and airport. But the most amusing aspect is that all those involved in staging this melodrama were specially recruited artists, architects, actors, and even circus performers, and all were duly honored for their contribution in saving Western democracy. If Hitler remains no more than a bad memory, this will be partly due to FUSAG and its masterstroke of military theatricals, which so terrified the children of the swastika with its compelling deception through a remarkably serious piece of military shamming. So that sooner or later, alongside *Saving Private Ryan*, there will be *Shamming Private Ryan*, an essential complement to the first production.

Europe saved by theater? It doesn't seem possible, but it's true. And it demonstrates that deception is not always bad. There are cases in which the innate capacity for pretense can even become a job that assures you a living for the rest of your days. Which is what happened to a man called Henri Louis Grin. But let us begin in England in 1921.

In the wet June of that year there was no great mood for laughter on the muddy streets of London. The news from India reported the growing stir around a man called Mahatma Gandhi. Who knew? Sooner or later England might have to give up its whole colony. This was more or less the message from the newspaper headlines thrown down by a foul-tempered official in the

Office for the Registry of Deaths. He was therefore in no mood for practical jokes when a woman of sixty-five appeared before him, tightly wrapped in a wet shawl with an ugly brown fringe. To say she spoke in a quiet voice would be an understatement: she held her words between her teeth as though they were gems from the Taj Mahal so that the official was forced to ask her at least three times to repeat the name of the deceased. Only at the third attempt could he finally make it out: "I've come to report that Henri Louis Grin has passed away."

He lowered his spectacles to take a closer look at her.

She nodded. And it was then that the office echoed with a contagious laugh: no one would believe that Grin was actually dead. Not at all. It had to be yet another of his inventions.

That's right, for had the gentleman in question ever done anything that anyone could be sure about? Even his death had to be yet another publicity stunt to be sold around the British Empire.

The woman remained calm, opened her rain-drenched shawl, and produced a small slip of paper on which a certain Dr. Banting of Southwark had certified the fatal consequences of a myocardial arrest. So was it true? Had the greatest liar on Earth really closed his eyes forever?

The official was tempted to believe her. Then he had second thoughts. Would a man like Grin have any difficulty forging a doctor's certificate? This Dr. Banting might not even exist; perhaps it was the name of a candle merchant or the latest fruit vendor in Neal's Yard market. That was probably it. The official put his spectacles back down and shook his head to signify his refusal. He would issue no document for fear of becoming the laughingstock of all London.

For her part, the woman was evidently prepared—if you're

related to the man who had been fooling public opinion for years, you don't expect anyone to believe you just like that. She put a hand inside her threadbare coat and pulled out a grainy photograph.

The man on the other side of the screen shuddered: the photo immortalized—in every sense—the deathbed of a perfect looka-like of Grin, his mouth half open and his eyes staring at the ceiling.

There was silence between the two parties.

It was interrupted by the woman, who, fortified by the photo-graphic evidence she had produced, spoke in a vaguely pious tone: "Henri Louis Grin passed away last night."

Could he believe her?

Of course, the photograph said it all. The eyes of the man who lay on the pillows seemed lifeless, lost as they were in a cosmic void. It was hard to dispute. All the more since Grin's face wasn't easily forgotten—it had been in all the papers when he went under the name of Louis de Rougemont (for he had lied to the world about his name too). There was no doubt the face was his. But all the same, damnation, this was the greatest liar ever seen on the banks of the Thames. Could he rely on a doctor's certificate and an unauthenticated photograph? Might it be a brother who looked very similar? Or his father? The official scratched his wide bald forehead, which made him look so much like Gandhi and annoyed him each time he saw it in the mirror. He poured him-self some water, then with the hint of a threat he asked: "Where's the body?"

The woman looked puzzled and mumbled an address in the docks area, on the other side of the river.

"So be it—I'll come and see for myself" was the drastic re-sponse of the official, determined not to be fooled.

They walked quite some distance in the pouring rain, in perfect silence, not looking at each other.

On the way, the official couldn't help but remember the day, twenty years before, when the most shameful charade ever known had been exposed in the English press. He remembered it very well, for he himself was an admirer of Louis de Rougemont, that man who had traveled the world, explored deserts and forests, ending up as a prisoner of Anangu witch doctors or fighting unarmed against ferocious beasts. Accounts of his adventures, mixtures of anthropological rigor and exotic charm, were published in the authoritative *Wide World Magazine*. Rougemont was a remarkable man, one of those people who could convince anyone, brightening their dull existence with the brightness of his own genius. It's a talent of no small importance—what generally produces envy and disdain can sometimes become a cause for idolatry. This is how it was with Grin: his exploits were universally followed, saving clerks and schoolmistresses from the suffocating banality of their monotonous everyday lives devoid of any excitement beyond the accidental death of their neighbor's cat. How could he not be adored? Guinea, the inhospitable country in his diaries, had become the exciting and adventurous Eden of a stupefied humanity longing as never before to thrill at the mere possibility of a different, exciting life filled with real emotions that at last gave meaning to the period of time between birth and death that seemed like a mere succession of bureaucratic milestones. He certainly lived it to the full—he described how he'd been held hostage for thirteen years by a godless tribe whose rituals, language, lore, and customs he recounted in scientific detail, claiming also to be a colleague of Alfred Gibson, the explorer who died in the Australian desert that later was given his name. Except that Gibson was a real anthropologist, an Aboriginal explorer infinitely less famous and less vain than Rougemont. For in the end, in modern society, where most people live a life unworthy of any mention, success came not from ability itself but from the capacity to flaunt it. Rougemont was a master in this respect, and England had celebrated him for years. He enjoyed immense popularity; his fame made him one of London's most renowned anthropologists. Children playing in the street pretended to ride on turtles in Borneo, and their mothers would meanwhile fret at the idea of that valiant hero at the mercy of bloodthirsty equatorial tribes. For his part, the king of Guinea was not averse to such a noble status; he felt he shouldered a mission that he didn't propose to ignore—if his readers wanted him to embody the illusion of a modern Heracles, he would give them what they wanted. There again, aren't all of us searching for some lie that gives our lives direction? Morally we condemn lying, we teach children about the virtue of telling the truth, but in the end we all know very well that objectivity is a dismal pond, a stark room, a bare tree: the richness of human experience is found in the imagination of novelists, in the magic of legends, in the distortion of art that becomes sublime only when it breaks away from the confines of reality. People criticize liars, but they carve statues to poets, to visionaries, to the Rougemonts of every age who, through their very act of lying, put us in touch with the galactic infinity of human creativity. What would we be without lies? A microscope on truth to pull it apart at every moment, recognizing that we are condemned to be infected by it? Or a telescope always pointing at the astral void to remind us how we resemble minuscule bacteria on the last of the planets? Science is disarming. Luckily, there are impostors who can save us from it.

But it just so happened that the scientific community didn't think the same way when a witness swore that the person in a photograph of Rougemont was in fact a Swiss charlatan by the name of Henri Louis Grin, a practiced cheat and fraudster, faithless husband and born impostor, capable more than anything else of building a life based solidly on lies. Forget Guinea, forget Alfred Gibson! After working as a warehouseman and a cook, Rougemont had spent years hoodwinking the scientific community—and thousands of readers too. Welcome to the glorious realm of Daloney Land.

This was shocking to the British. The man who had taken them light-years away from reality was wallowing in the mud of deceit, and nothing is more heinous than to feel yourself fooled by your own dreams. His readers had gazed at the whole of human experience through his eyes, but everything had turned out to be fake, a colossal fiction woven with a mixture of cunning and malice. And love turned to hatred. A hatred not directed at Grin: instead, they hated the reality that had ultimately humiliated and overwhelmed them.

When the official and the woman arrived at the humble house that was rotting in the damp air from the canal, a small crowd had gathered at the front door. The door creaked open, allowing them into a single blackened space at the end of which the corpse awaited them.

The man moved forward amid the sound of purling rain and tears. He was struck by the colorful circus-style poster, fixed to one wall, that proclaimed, KING LIAR: ENTERTAINMENT BY THE GREATEST LIAR EVER. Exactly. Because Grin's wondrous adventure had ended in the most unexpected way: after enduring an initial period of resentment, the master impostor felt himself surrounded by an entirely new kind of admiration. Those who had followed his adventures for years felt hurt and upset at discovering they had been false, but at the same time they couldn't help but appreciate his remarkable imagination. England had lost a cheat, and yet—paradoxically—it then called for him to return, as if to say: "We know you're a liar, that you've deceived us, but the truth is we want to be deceived. So please go back to telling your stories."

And so it was that Grin, without having to apologize in the slightest for his foolery, built a new identity for himself as a fairground phenomenon, boasting he was the greatest liar that Europe would ever see. His was a self-proclaimed monument to deceit. And therefore, exposed in front of everyone as a liar, not only was there no need to hide it but he was soon onstage wearing the crown of King Liar.

If the show didn't continue to the end of his life it was only because his true identity as Henri Louis Grin was no longer a secret. His youthful transgressions soon caught up with him, along with vast debts and financial frauds, plus a legion of abandoned lovers. If it hadn't been for these past peccadilloes, King Liar would have happily continued to profit from his lies, for which he was paid handsomely. Instead, among torn curtains and rat droppings, he was a king who died in poverty.

Who died, yes. For the man in the bed was certainly Grin, and he was certainly dead. The official checked his pulse at least four times before signing the document. After which the corpse was put into a coffin and buried before evening.

It is said that certain skeptical individuals took turns keeping watch at his grave for several days, for they knew that playing dead was not just a matter for zoologists: if there was a way of stealing the opossum's secret, King Liar would no doubt have worked it out.

Knowing how to lie, after all, had been his special trick through-out his life.

> **Liarism**—*noun*. Derived from King Liar, nickname for Henri Louis Grin (1847–1921). *Indicates a crazy need to be tricked, deceived, even swindled for the purposes of a glorious deception, a hundred times more magical than dull and petty reality.*

Related:

> **Fusagery**—*noun*. Derived from the acronym FUSAG, First United States Army Group. *Denotes a redeeming and providential charade, through which it is possible to obtain an undoubted advantage for oneself or others. In other words, fusagery is that kind of lie that saves your life. Or maybe the world.*

M

Mapuchize

WE HAVE ALWAYS BEEN TAUGHT THAT THOUGHTS live in the brain, whereas emotions come from the heart. The Greek fathers of medicine, from Hippocrates onward, made it perfectly clear that the images in our mind take form thanks to the activity of the brain, and this discovery marked the beginning of a slow process of discrediting the heart as the exclusive dwelling place of human nature. Until then, for centuries and centuries, it was believed that every feeling—rational and emotional—was enclosed inside the chest rather than the skull, and it is no coincidence that tribal ritual in war provided that the heart of the dead enemy was to be eaten, to appropriate his courage and his bravery. This is understandable since the heart, after all, is the seismograph of life itself; if it stops beating, then everything stops, just as the quickening and slowing of its rhythm go at the same pace as our fluctuations of feeling. However, modern-day neuroscience recognizes that the heart muscle is much more intelligent than we might imagine, since over two-thirds of it consists of neuron cells, which is like saying that it also thinks and reacts somehow to external stimuli.

Well, when I refer to this unexpected rationality of the heart, it's because a large part of what pertains to our interpersonal relationships seems to take form in that very place. As this is a dictionary, let us think especially about the words we use to define our relations with others: *discord*, *concord*, and, above all, *cordiality*. These are all nouns that contain *cor*, the Latin for *heart*: *discord* is literally the divergence of two hearts, just as *concord* is the meeting of two hearts, while *cordiality* is without doubt the opening of one's breast to another's feelings in an aura of positivity that seems to exclude envy and resentment. But if each one of us exists physiologically thanks to our heart, and *cordiality* is this pure, unblemished warmth, then where does the seed of hatred come from? Evidently not from the heart but from the mind, the Gomorrah of calculation, whose claims to superiority generate the most destructive conflicts. And indeed, on closer inspection, even in Greek mythology the goddess Atë, personification of disharmony, had the strange characteristic of not walking on the ground like all of her companions on Olympus—Atë circled in the air, over our heads, staring down at humanity, and from that eternal pedestal she orchestrated conspiracies and injustice among her subordinates. As if to say that trouble could never arise between those of equal heart, and yet when someone—or a part of us—takes a higher position, then it produces a sinister imbalance. Or even, if you like, a pathological imbalance. The Utku people in the far north of Canada, for example, teach their children that anger must be avoided like a physical sickness that requires treatment. In their social system, if anyone begins to feel anger toward

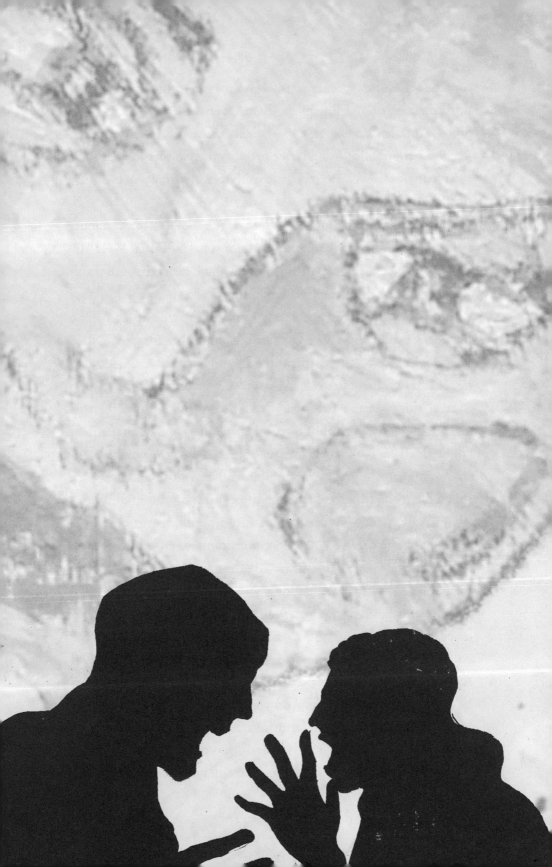

someone else, they spontaneously leave for a certain period of time until their natural feeling of goodwill is restored. The Mapuche of South America stand poles apart from the Utku in every sense, not just geographically, and it's worth taking a closer look at their surprising example, if only to avoid rousing their notoriously deadly anger.

It's the year of our Lord 1536 and we are about to make a journey through Peru to the Chilean region of Araucanía. Over the previous years a mighty Spanish army had pushed south from Panama in search of the legendary El Dorado. It was led by two ruthless warriors, Francisco Pizarro and Diego de Almagro. The first passed into history as the famous conquistador of the Inca Empire, but we are more interested in the second, whom Pizarro humiliated with a lesser role. Almagro never forgave him.

And this was the fuse that fired the cannon, since there is always some remote inkling of injustice in those who are then condemned to curse their own existence. Almagro was a small, stocky man of unprepossessing appearance whose features were much blemished by the first expeditions among the insalubrious islands of Ecuador—indeed he lost an eye, and it was only by a miracle that he survived infection, monsoons, assorted snakebites, and thousands of native arrows. All the same, he didn't give up. It could be said that the goddess Atë, circling above, had sown an unhealthy seed of revenge, such as to turn him to chronic violence, frayed by an unquenchable thirst for conquest. But what conquest? He and Pizarro had crushed the wealthy empire of Atahualpa. They now shared a vast power, which until then must have seemed unimaginable. And yet Almagro was tormented by a sense of frustration that urged him never, never, never to stop. It wasn't greed; it was much worse. Certain people spend their whole lives wandering about with no clear destination: theirs is a chaotic floundering, a hundred times more tiring than swimming, where everything is condensed into laying claim to something about which they know nothing and wish to know nothing because it's enough for them to rant and rave that it's not there. They might tell themselves that they've missed something, and in this delirium they glimpse a shadow of their own existence. Such people are reduced to bestiality without being any more animal than we all are, our instincts generally leading us to satisfy our obvious and basic needs. Almagro, on the other hand, seemed like a spinning top in the hands of one of those capricious young children who yell for the sake of yelling, regardless of whether they are tired or hungry. Well, exactly. He had been yelling for years without making a sound and had become dazed by the deafening echo of that yelling inside his skull, passing sleepless nights thinking up the worst anathemas against himself, against Pizarro, against accursed Peru and the wretched human condition. If he had been an Inuit, his isolation from the Utku would have been banishment for life. Goodwill was now alien to him, having become a war machine with no other purpose than to use his power and his gold to achieve a status almost divine, total and unreachable. It was in this frame of mind that he headed south in 1536 from the city of Cusco, to where he expected to find civilizations even more magnificent and opulent than those already conquered.

What a shame that his route through Chile was not one of the easier routes. He had to cross the cordillera of the Andes with glaciers and cliffs almost impassable for an expedition that included hordes of *Indios* and African porters, dozens of whom were dying. But Almagro was hell-bent on continuing, even when the horses sank into the snow, frozen up to their hocks. Hadn't he survived the pestilential jungles of Ecuador and Bolivia? Was a little snow going to stop him now? Onward! His obstinacy was unparalleled. He pushed ahead, against all and everything, with vexatious tenacity, literally incapable of uttering the word *enough*. Seemingly, though, it paid off. In June 1536 he finally saw the splendid lush valley of the Mapocho River spread beneath him, more delightful than Eden, stretching out like a welcome embrace in exactly the place where Chile's capital, Santiago, would one day stand. I like to think Almagro smiled that day. His stubbornness gave him at least as much to be pleased about as the brute force of his army, and from then on he could be proud of both. Had he not wrestled with life and finally won? He was thrilled at the thought that perhaps he had: he could get down from his horse and, for the first time in many years, cast his eyes over what creation really offered him.

But the story I'm telling just so happens to be about relative points of view. It's like in the food chain, where each time a carnivore sinks his teeth into a gazelle, there's always a larger predator lying in wait, ready to devour him. Here too there's a question of different levels—who is above, who is below—which brings us back to the goddess Atë, who is never our equal. It's about hierarchies. So Diego de Almagro could never have imagined, during those garish days of triumph, that he wasn't the only one into whose ear the goddess Atë was whispering ideas about superiority. There's always someone else, in the same neighborhood, who tunes in to the same radio frequency and is ready to pick up the gauntlet.

And what a gauntlet.

Enter here the Mapuche, warriors with a moral outlook that was rather different from that of the Utku. They were, let us say, more like those Amazonian tribes that regard displays of anger as a badge of supremacy, and even urge fathers and sons to indulge in daily bouts of yelling and fighting. Talk about the diversity of human customs: in this respect, the Mapuche provide quite an eloquent example of how to barter blood for bile. I doubt that Almagro had even heard of them, and yet they had lived for centuries on the banks of the Itata River, where the current eases before it joins the muddy waters of the Ñuble. No foreigner had ever disturbed them, and maybe this was why the Mapuche considered themselves unrivaled—meaning unbeatable—among all indigenous tribes. And with this tacit certainty they marshaled all their forces to await the arrival of the Spaniards. Bows, arrows, catapults. In their own way, they were well equipped.

For his part, Almagro was calmly oblivious. Calmness was something he hadn't encountered so far, and it rather terrified him, keeping him awake at night in his desperate search for something to curse. He would return to sleep only after telling himself that Chile was now his. He could call it Almagria if he wished. Whoever would have thought that an indigenous peril awaited him on the way toward the Strait of Magellan.

Almagro instructed one of his officers to patrol the territory to the south with a few hundred soldiers; he did not accompany them. The Mapuche outnumbered them almost tenfold. And the effects were catastrophic, for the battle had a psychological impact on the Spaniards far more devastating than the Andean glaciers. The atmosphere in Almagro's camp suddenly changed. Desertions and mutinies began, and the expedition was forced to head back to Peru. Almagro stopped sleeping once again: he spent his nights thinking up the worst anathemas against himself, the Mapuche, Pizarro, accursed Chile, and the wretched human condition.

You will say: a fine lesson for the little man's stubborn intransigence. Exactly, if it weren't for the fact that the Mapuche were far worse than anyone else when it came to losing their tempers, and they paid for it. For them, that day on the Itata River was just the start of a relentless war against the Spanish, known in history as the Arauco War. It all began when the stocky little one-eyed man came down from Cusco with the insatiable urge for conquest. Well, the Mapuche battled on for 345 years, giving the history books the longest war humanity has ever known.

Try to imagine what three and a half centuries of military conflict between an indigenous population and a great empire actually means. I reckon that Atë, to the displeasure of the gods of Olympus, must have moved to the Andes for good, taking out a Chilean passport. Otherwise it's impossible to explain how fourteen generations of fathers and sons could have continued tirelessly fighting on, and on, and on. History lost count of the number of attempts to make the Mapuche see reason with offers of peace: each time their stubbornness was unyielding, even though the war had forced them to sacrifice all they had. There's an endless list of their generals, called *toque*—which in the Mapudungun language means "he who fights with the ax"—to remind us that the Spanish fired cannons while their opponents brandished axes blessed by shamans. But it's wrong to think that any allowance was made for such disparity or that the Mapuche sought any more favorable treatment from their enemy: the Arauco War was fought with no holds barred, following the formula of *guerra a muerte*, taking no prisoners, killing all, right to the bitter end. Reading the history of those three and a half centuries of battles is like finding oneself in front of an *Iliad* squared: it recounts successive acts of unprecedented violence, fortresses destroyed and rebuilt, smallpox epidemics, Spanish governors slaughtered, and indigenous warriors impaled in front of their troops. Around a hundred thousand Mapuche were killed. The number of Spanish casualties was around half that, and then there was the Chilean regular army. A bloodbath.

All in the name of a furious defense of boundaries and the right to do as you wish in your own home; all out of a stubborn urge for supremacy between two rival groups, entirely different in culture, in origin, and even in their political unit of measure. Who knows whether either side—between episodes of attack, revenge, and retreat—ever paused to ask whether it was worth all the trouble. And who knows if there was anyone, when the war finally came to an end, who missed the adrenaline rush of battle. What is certain is that some wars go far beyond what seems to be at stake. They end up being seen by those who are fighting them as a metaphor for life itself, in which surrender is never an option. It is our heartbeat, our alpha and our omega; it ends up becoming all one with the ticking of time itself and the beating of the war drum. It seems like yesterday that some-one fired the first shot. And yet the hair under your helmet has turned gray, and like the Mapuche, for 345 years, your days and your energies have been turned to dust.

It all fits: three of the sisters of the goddess Atë were called Age, Pain, and Regret.

One of her brothers, I would suggest, was Time Wasted.

> **Mapuchize**—*transitive verb.* Derived from the long Arauco War, fought by the Mapuche and colonial Spaniards between 1536 and 1881. *Describes a particular and extreme form of dedication to a cause or to a question of principle, so that it develops into an all-out conflict. Therefore, expressions like "to Mapuchize a family argument or a disagreement between colleagues" describes the transformation of the dispute into bitter, perpetual, full-blown, and practically irresolvable hostility.*

Nazinate

THERE IS SATAN IN ALL OF US. WHETHER WE LIKE IT OR not, we are capable of causing hatred, shame, revenge, and deliberately stooping to the most despicable levels of evil. Religions speak of it as the darkness of sin, countered by the light of revelation. And yet in the very beginning there was a competition over which shone most brightly. After the sun and the moon, in third place was Venus, the third brightest celestial body to appear in our sky, visible in the first light of day. Therefore it has been known since ancient times as the Morning Star, and the divinity connected to it was called Lucifer, which means "bearer of light." In classical times this luminous planet seemed to threaten the divine preeminence of the sun, so it was hallowed as a symbol of conflict, of division (it is no coincidence that *devil* means "he who separates"). Judeo-Christian tradition added the rest: Lucifer was the prince of the rebel angels, then was renamed

Satan. Around him would be gathered all those who from the very beginning didn't want to fall into line, including the god of greed, Mammon (Hebrew for "hidden treasure"), and the terrible Beelzebub ("lord of the flies," of sicknesses that lead to death, covered with insects), without forgetting the legendary Lilith, who preceded Eve as Adam's first wife but whom he rejected because she refused to submit to him. This assorted club of demons would keep watch over all that we label *evil*, leaving aside the fact that evil has a multiplicity of faces. It most commonly shows itself when our bestial side gains the upper hand, refusing to accept the measure of reason, the slowness of persuasion, the

progressive development of mutual discussion. In short, though Lucifer is no watchmaker, it is primarily a question of time: explanation is a long business, while attack is immediate, instantaneous, seemingly advantageous, precisely because it is physical and direct. Human beings are well able to resolve their differences, working out compromises and curbing their prejudices, but each of these strategies requires effort, energy, and tolerance. Otherwise, the satanic way beckons temptingly, aiming straight for a result, rendering anyone in the way an obstacle to be swept aside. Evil is born here—fundamentally through impatience. It is what happens in conflicts between states, when the military route replaces the slower and more nuanced path of diplomacy. After all, in linguistic terms, an insult is nothing more than a sound used to express complicated states of mind without too much beating about the bush: when we swear at someone, we are simply trying not to waste time, expressing our growing rancor in a message that comes through loud and clear. If this warning—which is often equivalent to a threat—isn't heeded by the recipient, then an identical process leads us to dispense with formalities, moving this time into action. Evil isn't simply a degeneration: it is often the most convenient way of resolving a conflict, and as such is always based on an identical lie, that of having exhausted every other alternative to avoid the worst. Forget the horns and the goat's feet; hatred and bad-mouthing serve well in cutting through the delays, getting straight down to business.

This is true, however, for all those occasions in which there's a dispute, when something is at stake: once this is resolved, hostilities generally come to an end. But what happens if evil emerges like the gratuitous, spectacular, and devastating eruption of a volcano, totally independent of any personal interest? What happens if the injury inflicted doesn't involve you winning any war or contest but simply taking pleasure at the sight of an open wound? Here indeed the situation becomes more complicated, for we touch on the crucial point of so-called abomination, a genuine abandonment of the human sphere. And then, yes, the almanac of biblical demons may be useful: many figures such as Moloch, Belphegor, and Azazel come from pagan, Assyrian, and Phoenician cults, where they received human sacrifices and embodied anger, violence, fury. In other words, they offered a face and a name to those terrible human episodes in which we allow ourselves to fall into the vortex of absurd, depraved violence that has no purpose other than the enjoyment of a false omnipotence. Demons were corrupt beings, all tongue, teeth, claws, and deformed bodies, as if to emphasize that they were not a part of humanity: their bestiality fed on bestiality itself.

You will say: relics of ancient barbarism.

And yet no. On the contrary, our paths are full of Beelzebubs and Asmodeuses; we come across them in fast-food joints and shopping malls, as well as when we see ourselves in the mirror. Immersion in evil is such a common experience in our stupefying everyday city lives: there's a silent part of us that chooses to reveal the worst of itself, doggedly searching for nothing more than a shot of adrenaline, the momentary illusion of escaping from any moral criterion, deciding other people's fate. God, what a laugh! Is the ticket worth the price or not? In moments of boundless hatred, we feel ourselves promoted to the rank of judges, if not divinities.

Okay, there's no actual bloodshed; no one murders their fellow human being behind the hedges in the park like Jack the Ripper. But is it worth it? Nowadays, staining your hands with blood would just be extremely bad form, not to say unhygienic, since everyone is obsessed with continually cleansing themselves of microbes and bacteria. Human sacrifices are now performed instead through sterile, aseptic ritual. In the third millennium, when every life is first of all a virtual narrative, to witness bloodshed all you have to do is go online—the god Baal revels in his orgies of gratuitous violence, while Moloch never misses the chance to instill deadly rage in anyone who approaches the precincts of his temple. There's no real reason here to let our own hounds loose: all we have to do is drink from the spring of eternal spite, unaware that what we are doing is actually dragging ourselves down" (another biblical demon, Belial, was described as "the god that never rises again"). It's a mistake to offer any hint of criticism: descent into the depths offers no reprieve.

If I must look for some reference to the past, I can find nothing more fitting than what happened in the 1930s in central Siberia, in that godforsaken place that was the camp at Nazino. There, for at least two weeks, the worst of the worst prevailed among the human species, with no one feeling any need to curb their brutality. On the contrary: there was a rejoicing at the abyss, and a feeling that the bounds of legality had been crossed, so that during those infamous days—whatever they might be called—I think Mephistopheles, Belphegor, Beelzebub, and all the others must have been holding Soviet passports. It's no coincidence that during the events I'm about to describe, Mikhail Bulgakov was working tirelessly in his house in Moscow, writing *The Master and Margarita*, where everything was a frantic whirl of devils and demons. Unbeknown to the author, they were busy at Nazino too.

It had all begun about a year before when two eager officials arrived to see Stalin with a revolutionary plan. That morning, comrades Jagoda and Berman were in an optimistic mood. They watched the leader leaf through their file of papers, not missing a single expression. When he reached the last word, their anticipation was at its peak. Stalin stood up and moved to the window. Seeing him so upright against the external light made him look much taller, though it was well known that he ordered anyone making a statue of him to add a few inches.

"I don't like extravagant solutions. I find them annoying, for when they go wrong you find yourself with twice as many difficulties," Stalin said, tracing his finger down the edge of the curtain.

"Ah, but in this case, everything is assured!" Comrade Berman hastened to reply. It was his task to oversee the gulags, and he would have willingly listed five or six good reasons if Comrade Jagoda, chief of police, hadn't hurried to interpose: "In truth, I think I can add something to what has been written. Thanks to this project, we will sweep crime from Moscow and Leningrad." And he smiled, as though he had already swept it away.

"So let's hear: how will you do it?" Stalin asked with a mixture of irritation and impatience. Comrade Jagoda couldn't ask for more: "A convoy of trains from Moscow, and one from Leningrad. We'll fill them not just with peasants left with no land but also with criminals, rapists, murderers—in other words, the whole prison population. And once we've packed them all into wagons—"

Comrade Berman couldn't resist sounding the final note of triumph, so he interrupted Jagoda with unusual excitement: "At that point bye-bye. We'll send them all to Tomsk!"

Jagoda didn't respond. Instead, he took a step forward, forcing himself now to adopt the calm manner of a strategist: "In this way, Comrade Stalin, we will resolve three problems: we'll give new land to the peasants, we'll empty the prisons, and most of all, out of nothing, we'll create a fine town in the heart of Siberia."

Stalin made not the slightest sound, either of agreement or disagreement. He stood quite still for ten minutes or so, making strange movements with his boots as though he were gathering dust in order to push it under the carpet. No surprise. Each comrade has his own way when it comes to reaching a decision. Suddenly he seemed to shudder, moved across to the desk, and stamped and signed the file of papers. It was done. All was made ready. A few weeks later, with perfect Soviet efficiency, the stations of Moscow and Leningrad were teeming with passengers waiting to leave, guarded by the police and by the army. There were all types among that mass of people: old peasants with calloused hands, girls wrapped in shawls with babies around their necks, kids fooling around irritating rough-nosed prisoners the likes of whom had never before been seen, men who were doubtless more familiar with the sword than with the spade. Crowded onto those platforms was the whole criminal labor force of the Soviet capitals. But in just the same way as wine is diluted with water, likewise the dregs of society had been diluted with several thousand wretches from the countryside, people who had been left with no field to farm because someone had taken it to build the usual factory.

What a strange gathering, bystanders thought.

A real social experiment, those in charge pondered, genuinely puzzled. But there was no going back now. The convoys left on May 1, 1933, and would reach their destination nine days later. And it was here, when they arrived, that the problems began.

Quite simply, they had been overly optimistic in imagining that the camp already set up would be enough to hold everyone. In the end, there was no room for at least five thousand, all of them criminals, since the peasants had hurried off immediately to take possession of the land. What could be done? Sending them back home was out of the question.

Comrades Jagoda and Berman therefore decided to take their inspiration from Stalin: to lift the carpet and sweep the dust underneath, come what may. After all, no one was worried about the fate of five thousand convicts. Full steam ahead!

On May 18, 1933, the deportees were packed onto large barges moored on the Ob River. After several days they would be unloaded at Nazino, where a makeshift camp was waiting for them in the middle of nowhere. They would remain there for the rest of their days. To work the land? Hopefully. Not least because there were barely twenty tons of flour on the boats, after which everyone would starve. Or rather, not everyone. Only the deportees, seeing that the guards carried guns.

This was how the inferno of Nazino began.

What happened in that camp is one of the lowest points that man has ever reached, proving how evil can sometimes spread like a rampant virus. Food supplies ran out in less than three days, when the first cases of cannibalism began in the makeshift penal colony. The guards did nothing to stop it, watching the social experiment with relish. According to survivors, no one worked the land, no one attempted to fish—the fighting was continual and the butchered corpses were turned into food. The regression, which went well beyond the animal stage, even saw deportees used like hunting dogs, rewarded with scraps of meat if they plunged into the icy Ob to bring river birds back to shore. After another twenty days, every kind of epidemic broke out among the cannibals of Nazino, until it pleased Beelzebub and his followers to spread typhoid too. Over four thousand died.

One thing is sure: the human race is not unacquainted with evil.

Nazinate—*intransitive verb.* Derived from the massacre at Nazino in southwest Siberia (1933). *Describes the actions of someone who yields gratuitously to his basest instincts, allowing his most loathsome parts to emerge.*

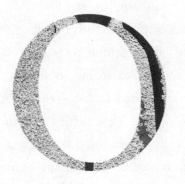

Oatism
and **Olivarism**

WHAT ARE WE PREPARED TO DO IN THE NAME of work? How far are we willing to push ourselves in an imaginary race to prove our efficiency and productivity? In 2013, a young Japanese television executive died from a heart attack after she aimed for a record of two hundred hours of overtime in a month. A latter-day Stakhanov in a kimono? I don't think so. For much has changed since the times of the legendary Russian miner. Technology allows us to be available at any moment, in any place, so the fixed surroundings of the workplace no longer exist, nor the old fixed-hour system. What's more, competition is more intense, so the salary is only one factor in play, along with the dopamine rush we get from winning a place on the podium.

And yet once upon a time, many years ago, there was a world in which work was there to provide us with a living. We farmed the land or put our manual skills to good use purely out of the practical need to support ourselves: work produced an income, and the income was transformed into food (no coincidence that it's called a *salary*, from the Latin *salarium*, the sum paid to Roman soldiers for salt). The modern world seems to have totally forgotten these real—I would even say biological—origins. The only objective now is money: more important even than the worker's life itself.

And indeed thousands of people in Indonesia wear their lives out in a true inferno of toxic fumes. Crowded around the incandescent crater of a volcano, they extract slabs of sulfur from a boiling pit. Most of them don't last more than ten years, destroying first their eyesight, then their lungs, for which they get around seven dollars a day.

Clandestine high-tech scavengers make even less at the Guiyu garbage dump in the Chinese province of Guangdong, where thousands of tons of electronic debris ends up. Groups of women and children work away among waste batteries, effluent, half-corroded microchips, and rusty metal to separate copper from lithium, storing five times the normal level of carcinogenic lead in their bloodstreams.

Far better paid, on the other hand, are the crab fishermen in the Bering Strait between Alaska and Siberia: the terms of their contracts specifically provide for compensation in the event of death or permanent incapacity, a prospect that is taken for granted since

2

3

these are treacherous waters with twenty-meter-high waves and temperatures so low that sea foam freezes instantly (nine out of ten fishermen suffer fatal accidents).

Yes, you will say: that's the price of consumerism. We are prepared to let people risk their lives just so we can have crab claws on our supermarket shelves. Sure, that's how it is: people have always played down the moral and environmental consequences of the profit-spinner of the moment. In the nineteenth century, to protect the sugar plantations of Hawaii from rats, hundreds of Javan mongooses were imported, with the result that they killed not only the rodents but many other kinds of animal, destroying the livelihoods of farmers and breeders. This is the cruel—but also idiotic—law of personal interest to which the modern age has sacrificed everything. What troubles me, however, is the ease with which people have been prepared to turn themselves into a business commodity.

In China, among less affluent classes, there's a growing practice for people to sell portions of their own existence via *ding zui*, namely the mechanism by which wealthier people hire someone to go to prison on their behalf. Many family breadwinners, for an agreed price, have been prepared to give up their own freedom in order to serve someone else's sentence. Some have even sacrificed their lives, allowing themselves to be executed on the assurance of an appropriate payment to their family, further increased if the execution is followed by the sale of organs on the black market. There again, trafficking kidneys and corneas is a thriving business in many Far Eastern slums, from Kathmandu to the shantytowns of Mumbai and Karachi. But even closer to home, there's a growing number of people in prosperous Western economies who offer themselves for a few hundred euros per session as human guinea pigs for trials of drugs and chemical compounds. We are therefore at the exact opposite of "working to live"—people in the third millennium can perfectly well "work to die."

So, if I may, let us pause here. In the introduction we saw how at least three words connected to the notion of work came from the lives of particular people: *Stakhanovite, Oblomovist,* and *Luddite.* No word yet exists to indicate the disease of our time, this emotional dependence on work that is so strong it becomes an obsession, this dedication of body and soul to something that ought merely to provide us with a roof, clothing, and enough food to live on.

Yes, of course: there's the word *workaholic,* but let's go a little further back to the origin of the problem, not least because some interesting discoveries are to be found just around the corner.

The man who coined the word *workaholic* was an academic from Kentucky, Professor Wayne Oates. Isn't that enough to name a word after him? Yes, in theory, but one with a less obvious definition. Oates was born in 1917 into a family as poor as could be. His father worked like mad; his mother returned home each evening from a textile factory with her back in pieces. A few years earlier, Henry Ford had been relentlessly testing out his assembly line, and the US economy was booming to levels never imagined. But at what cost? In a New York garment factory 146 workers were burned to death, their fate sealed when the owners locked the doors to stop them going outside without permission. This was the cost.

In any event, when Wayne was abandoned by his father at a young age, he was brought up by a religious grandmother while his mother worked away at the loom to bring home a meager wage. For a boy of twelve in the late 1920s there weren't many choices: he was likely to spend his life working long hours in a factory, at the end of which he would emerge gray haired. And Wayne shuddered at the thought, feeling its approach each day like a real monster, and far worse than his nightmares, however much his grandmother frightened him with the plagues of Egypt and Aaron with the Golden Calf. Constantly prone to colds, wearing a secondhand overcoat several sizes too big, the boy changed the subject when anyone asked what he was going to be, well aware that what lay before him was the usual rise from errand boy to factory hand, and from factory hand to not much else. There are moments when everything appears before you with depressing clarity, and you'd give anything to convince yourself that your poor hovel might one day be a pretty villa. Wayne found himself in exactly this condition: he could count all the years to come, one by one, and could have penciled on his face the wrinkles of a life of drudgery. This was his plague of Egypt. And yet no. Providence, for which the old lady of the house had so fervently prayed, ordained that Wayne should have a different future. Just as the darkest storm clouds of the 1929 crisis were gathering, Wayne was selected from among the poor of the district and offered the chance to escape from a life of hardship and receive an excellent education at public expense and, who knows, perhaps even to find a good job. Hallelujah! Yet it remained to be seen what would become of the boy who continued to give thanks in church to the One who had blessed him from on high. He became a distinguished academic, a leading psychologist. But alongside his scientific interests he never lost his religious ardor, and even became a popular theologian.

When he died at a ripe old age, his son Charles described him as "an absolute, bustling dynamo of energy." And this is impossible not to recall when we think that it was he who coined the word *workaholic* in his best-known textbook. Professor Oates had known the working-class districts where the exploitation of labor forced human beings to work at a frantic pace. More than anything, he himself was afraid he would end up at a loom, but the hand of the Lord had led him to higher levels, where no one wears outsize overcoats and where people kid themselves that work is an intellectual mission, almost an expression of personal talent, if not indeed an enjoyment dressed up as a social duty. This had been a legacy of his years among battered stoves and washing lines, counting the potatoes on his plate. Humanity was divided between those who cursed their jobs and those who worked away with a smile. And yet I like to think that Wayne Oates, up there among professors and doctors, was about to grasp something fundamentally important. A worker can die from exhaustion (or because they locked her in to keep watch on her), but those in the elite club of top jobs can also die—no kidding—from having built an idol to their profession, like Aaron with the Golden Calf. Only a psychologist and religious educator could see this risk: the sanctification of work, even giving it a mystical status, looking to it for a total meaning of life. It's no coincidence that what Japanese doctors call *karoshi* ("death from overwork") is a disease that doesn't afflict porters and carpenters: the phenomenon of the professional river bursting its banks is to be found in offices, creative environments, graphic design studios, architectural practices, and universities. Namely in all those places where people can fall in love with what others regard as simply a job.

An eloquent symbol of this almost carnal passion for work is Gaspar de Guzmán, Count-Duke of Olivares, in seventeenth-century Spain. Some may have heard of him as a patron of Diego Velázquez, who painted several remarkable portraits of him. But with all due respect to that formidable artist, I think it's well worth talking about another aspect of this mighty dignitary. Olivares was larger than life, in every sense of the word: extravagant, unwilling to delegate, and a worthy exponent of the baroque period, he appeared to others as an ungainly pachyderm, voracious in appetite as well as ideas. Sometimes we encounter people whose only interest is in how others see them. For such individuals (and Olivares was a prime example) the world is a stage, and they imagine themselves continually called to strut upon its boards. Now, the point is that these personalities have an absolute need to pour their enormity into a container of equivalent size, wholly translating themselves into a role of exceptional importance. If this doesn't happen, it's a real problem, because they develop a tiresome sense of cosmic injustice, as if a pillar of physics had gone. This was how it was with Olivares: for the first thirty years of his life, while receiving the honors due to a young nobleman, no one deigned to reward him with any office commensurate with his own opinion of himself. So Gaspar chafed and snarled, absolutely and intimately certain that sooner or later he would be given some glorious appointment from which he would squeeze every ounce of satisfaction, retrospectively. This was his due, at the very least. So it came as no surprise when, one day, His Royal Highness King Philip III appointed him to look after the young prince, his heir. For Olivares, more than looking after the young boy, it was as if he himself had been crowned.

Then, to cap it all, the king died unexpectedly and the sixteen-year-old ascended the throne. The fat advisor grew fatter with pride, and with the excuse of helping the young king, still in the flush of youth, he took it upon himself to make all decisions. He was insatiable. It's enough to say that every nobleman was allowed just one title under Spanish law, and whenever he was promoted in title he had to renounce the previous one: Olivares persuaded the young king to appoint him duke but, having got what he wanted, declared that under no circumstances would he stop calling himself count. All the courtiers protested, of course, but he was marvelous at explaining why he deserved this and that. Moral of the story: he was the only person, out of everyone, to remain count and duke for life. And he accumulated offices with the same frantic fury that he is said to have eaten his meals, so that his presence at banquets was not to be encouraged. It is most odd that, over the years, Olivares developed a real fear of being cast aside. He knew the fickle moods of the courts, so he found it wise to be simply irreplaceable, taking the work of all ministers upon himself. He would supervise everything, from foreign policy to military strategy, from religious affairs to justice, from economics to upholding morality, without ignoring culture, festivals, or society life. At the age of fifty he began displaying signs of psychological stress. In order to work twenty hours a day, Olivares gave up sleeping, ordered his servants to keep him awake, and compensated for what he lost in sleep with sumptuous meals at all hours. He soon became uncontrollable. He attacked everyone, verbally and worse, shouted until he lost his voice, threatened his advisors and sometimes even the king, accusing him of casting him in the shade. Meanwhile he had a complete obsession about filling pages and pages of absurd reports as if to demonstrate to the world—and to himself—just how vital his work was. Olivares was going truly mad. He gave orders to build a vast palace, the Buen Retiro, which seemed to everyone like an excuse for him to make himself yet busier, even though a daughter and grandson had died without him offering them any solace. To those who accused him of letting them die with no concern for their suffering, he merely replied, "I had no time. I was required elsewhere," and to prove it he embarked on a rash fiscal scheme, revolutionizing the whole tax system. The whole of Spain began to hate him, and the king's circle spoke of him as a raving madman regularly afflicted by hallucinations. Eventually he was fired.

But even in exile at Zamora, close to the border with Portugal, now sick and losing his mind, Olivares was still doggedly at work: it is said he demanded a municipal appointment and proclaimed edicts at all hours on the grazing of cattle and tavern reforms. His last words, before he finally closed his eyes, are said to have been "Wake me early tomorrow morning."

Oatism—*noun.* Derived from the psychologist Wayne Edward Oates (1917–1999). *Denotes the transformation of a job into an object of worship, and therefore the religious celebration of ourselves not as human beings but as holders of a position.*

Olivarism—*noun.* Derived from Gaspar de Guzmán y Pimentel, Count-Duke of Olivares (1587–1645). *Describes the obsession of those who identify themselves only through* *their work, devoting every energy, thought, and emotion to it. The Olivarist will thus become incapable of forming any human relationship that is not in keeping with the exercise of his personal position.*

P

Parksian *and* Pietersonism

PRAISE BE TO THE BUS, FOREVER. AND PLEASE note, I mean the ordinary strap-hanging local bus and not the more comfortable railroad coach. In the end, they represent two kindred but entirely different worlds. The bus is for the city, for work, a clammy vehicle, whereas its cousin immediately brings to mind vacations, leisure, and with it all the comforts of air-conditioning. It's rather like seeing two relatives who look so alike but dress so differently and lead such different lives. There again, the railroad coach can boast in its DNA that it transported the coffin of Abraham Lincoln. Its inventor, George Mortimer Pullman, was fiendishly clever at marketing and pulled off the most sensational publicity coup of the nineteenth century to promote his luxury railroad cars designed as traveling drawing rooms. In other words, he turned the president's funeral into an advertising commercial. It seems incredible, but this was how the Pullman coach first appeared: as a hearse on rails, from Washington to Springfield. Considering that this was 1865, I would call it a marketing milestone. A thousand points to Mr. Pullman.

But here, with no disrespect to Abraham Lincoln, we'll be considering the humble bus. I don't imagine any head of state would wish to be carried to his grave on a number 25. Why? Because the bus is like a medieval torture device that has remained just the same over the ages, crystallized in its chronic discomfort, impervious to changing times and technological progress. Man will soon land on Mars, but public transport routes continue in their Homeric intent to forge the warrior soul. The bus requires you to develop a multiple resistance—to weather, to smells, and to fellow travelers. Taking for granted the frustrating lack of seats (a matter already ripe for philosophical study), you have to hold on tightly against the continual jolting while keeping a careful lookout for pickpockets. What you gain in return, however, is something rare: a deep awareness of tribal spirit. It's no surprise that the great film director Mario Monicelli claimed, with his characteristic irony, that the great age of comedy came to an end when scriptwriters and directors stopped using public transport. It was a most vivid way of describing the impossibility of portraying a country without actually sharing its excitements, its tensions, its ups and downs—in every sense. It is said that Winston Churchill would travel on public transport at the most crucial moments in English history to gauge the mood of the people, to eavesdrop on their discussions, to sound out their views. Perhaps it's just a legend,

but there is no doubt that buses, trams, and subway trains are the most powerful lenses through which to study what people really are. Of them all, the bus is the most all-pervading and the most austere, the only public transport vehicle that collects its passengers almost from their doorsteps, connecting the poorest suburbs to city-center stores, and bringing together—day in, day out, in a wondrous social alchemy—the eighty-year-old with his shopping basket and the teenager with her schoolbag covered with stickers, the timid immigrant and the stressed office worker who sleeps with her head against the window. Even in its name—this monosyllabic *bus*—there's the indelible mark of its very popularity as a vehicle.

It's worth explaining why.

In 1826, a certain Stanislas Baudry had invested all of his resources in the construction of a flour mill on the outskirts of Nantes, in northwest France, but since he was a restless man who could turn his hand to anything, he decided to expand the family business by opening a small bathing establishment heated with the water from the steam engine that powered the mill. And since he had a good nose for business, it proved an excellent idea, especially when Baudry invented a convenient transport service that carried customers from the city center to the entrance of his thermal baths. At first it was a simple, fairly large carriage, pulled by two horses, but everything began from this. Anyone wishing to relax in the miller's thermal baths knew there was a vehicle waiting outside the shop of a Monsieur Omnès, a hatter, and a man with sense of humor—years before he had fixed a sign over his shop with the Latin words *Omnes omnibus*, a pun on his name, meaning "Everything for everyone." What a coincidence! The fact that Baudry's carriage began its journey right in front of the sign meant that the service was soon commonly known as the *omnibus*. And it was on a bus that one of the most moving events in post–World War II America took place.

On December 1, 1955, Rosa Parks, a forty-two-year-old seamstress, was working at a department store in Montgomery, Alabama. Imagine her, this kindly looking woman with the smile of a schoolteacher, one of those people in life whom you never forget, whose birthday you always remember. Rosa was one of those extraordinary cases in which outer appearances don't reflect a person's inner fiber—to see her you would have said she was fragile, destined to collide with the voracious animal life of the human jungle. On the contrary, it was she who was the true jaguar.

As we know, daily life is a repetition of the same rituals, yet among these rituals lurks the seed of the unexpected. And it is there, at such moments, that the chain breaks, jamming the mechanism. Luigi Pirandello described it in *The Train Whistled*, in which a faithful employee suddenly recognizes the infinite emptiness of his daily routine, and thanks to the whistle of a train, he imagines the immense catalogue of all that he would never experience. How many trains whistle without anyone arriving at the same junction? Luckily, every so often there's someone who hears the whistle like an inescapable imperative, from which they find the strength to question everything.

On that day in 1955, Rosa Parks was waiting as always for the bus at the end of her work shift. She didn't yet know that very soon a train would in some way whistle for her too, tearing the curtain of normality that makes shamelessness possible. But let's leave Rosa for just a moment at the bus stop. We'll return to her very soon as she prepares to board the 2857 bus on Cleveland Avenue. In the meantime, we're going back another sixty-two years.

It is 1893, and we're in South Africa, on a train, in a first-class carriage. It's traveling quite normally, as it does each day, toward Pretoria. Some passengers are reading, others dozing. A young barrister with classic Indian features is taking notes on the papers for his latest commercial case: he is defending one of the leading companies in the Natal province. "Excuse me, sir—may I see your ticket?" a voice asks him in peremptory fashion. The young man doesn't look up from his work. He automatically takes the ticket from his inside jacket pocket, holding it up between two fingers.

"Would you follow me to the third class? You can't stay here."

"Sorry? Where should I follow you to?"

"To third class. This carriage is reserved for Western passengers."

"I've purchased a first-class ticket."

"Yes, I agree, the ticket office has made a mistake. You're not white."

It's a tough business arguing with a brilliant legal advocate. The exchange between the two becomes more heated for at least fifteen minutes, interrupted like the gong in a boxing ring by the sudden screech of brakes. The train comes to a halt; we're at Pietermaritzburg station. Strange—it doesn't normally stop at Pietermaritzburg. At this point two other railroad staff seize the young barrister by the arm. They push him toward the carriage door in spite of his most insistent protests and bundle him out. Lying on the ground in the locomotive's steam, the young man shouts for them to at least return his papers, and has barely finished the request before his papers shower down on him from the carriage window. The stationmaster blows his whistle, the engine driver gives a nod from the cabin, and the train resumes its journey while the barrister, angry and covered with dust, puts his papers back in order.

Well, that young lawyer was rather like the seamstress Rosa

Parks. Still only twenty-four, he was about to become acquainted with an unexplored part of himself, precisely because of the humiliation of that day. His name was Mohandas Gandhi, and he would transform the first-class seat denied him into a manifesto for an historic battle. Does this mean that until that day he had been blind to the injustices of South Africa? Not at all. But Pirandello's train hadn't whistled until then, opening his eyes once and for all. And Indian independence began to take form on that train traveling toward Pretoria.

Curiously, on December 1, 1955, in Alabama, a question over seating on public transport was about to urge Rosa Parks, just like Gandhi, to set in motion an unprecedented revolution. Trains and buses clearly are the cradles of civil rights. And so, having left Rosa at the bus stop, we now return to find her boarding the bus to take a seat in the center of the vehicle. These were the so-called mixed seats. Namely, those on which Black people could sit, except that they had to get up straightaway if a white person came along and there were no open seats. This is what happened after a few stops, and the driver told her to stand. For a Black American this was perfectly normal, but for Rosa that day, that was no longer the case. In other words, Pirandello's train had whistled, telling her she mustn't get up. She refused. At first the driver thought she was crazy. That's what always happens to anyone who hears the train whistle: it's assumed they are mentally unbalanced. But a few minutes of argument was enough to clarify that Rosa certainly wasn't out of her mind. The yellow, white, and green striped bus pulled up at the sidewalk and was soon surrounded by a crowd of onlookers: "What's going on up there? Pardon me, I can't see."

"There's a Black woman who won't leave her seat. She must have been feeling ill."

Yet Rosa Parks was feeling fine. Never felt better. Even when she was arrested for violating public bus segregation laws, it seemed to everyone that she was perfectly healthy. From that day, an all-out boycott began that would last for over a year. No Black person would board any bus in Montgomery until the authorities were compelled to repeal the public bus segregation law on the grounds that it was unconstitutional. Just see what a seamstress can do on a bus. So, while Pullman coaches can trace their glory back to the funeral of Lincoln, the man who abolished slavery, it can be said that the abolition of segregation laws was entirely due to a seat on a bus.

The bus boycott was certainly an odd one, but from time immemorial the most powerful protests have been the ones that happen when you least expect them: Gandhi in a first-class railroad car, Rosa Parks on a bus in Montgomery. This is why our dictionary cannot ignore Hector Pieterson, who at the age of twelve took a bus to school each day, in Soweto. He too was a citizen of color, born and destined to grow up under the shadow of apartheid. And when the National Party ordered all schools to teach the language of white people, a multitude of children like Hector invented the school strike: no one would go into class, no one would answer "Present" when the teacher called their name. The protest was all the louder because it came from a chorus of children, and maybe this was why it offended the authorities. In 1976, they sent armored cars onto the streets against a crowd of kids still in short trousers, and on June 16, Hector Pieterson was shot dead because he had dared, like many others, to listen to the Pirandellian train whistle, convinced they could make everything change. Maybe people could accept the idea of adults opening their eyes upon their own abyss, but a protest by children was inconceivable because it was a thousand times more inexorable. Adults can be bought off with self-interest; they generally submit to the code of silence that protects every system based on injustice. But Hector's position was different: there is nothing to weigh against the sense of injustice for someone who still interprets reality through the single parameter of the law of nature, according to which pain is simply pain, and those born are not born to suffer. That is why the soldiers were ordered out against the schoolchildren's protest in Soweto.

Gandhi and Rosa Parks lived at least to see the result of their battles, but not Hector, who sacrificed his life at twelve. His bus had reached the end of the line after just a few stops.

Parksian—*adjective.* Derived from Rosa Parks (1913–2005). *Describes a memorable victory for oneself or for others that grows out of a small gesture, from any minor detail that suddenly reveals to us how unendurable our position is.*

Pietersonism—*noun.* Derived from Hector Pieterson (1963–1976). *Denotes how any move for change, any urge for people to open their eyes, to recognize the true circumstances of their situation, is seen as a danger to the order of things. Because those who manage to see themselves or reality through the eyes of a child will not accept compromises. And this is the most inflammatory of viewpoints.*

Q

Questic

T
HE YEAR 1895 WAS CERTAINLY PIVOTAL: THE
Lumière brothers in Paris invented the cinematograph
while Guglielmo Marconi in Bologna was transmitting
radio waves. It would mark the beginning of the technological
revolutions that carried humanity into the dazzling modern age,
in which the distance between continents would be eliminated.
How exciting to be able to see India projected onto a screen or
to hear Congo drums on the radio. Truly amazing. But for the
moment, people had to make do with illustrated books. At best,
there were descriptions of those who had actually been to India or
Africa. Their readers had to trust them, believe them.

This was what Emilio Salgari did, the tenant of a humble up-
stairs apartment in a small northern Italian town, always bent
over his desk writing his adventure stories amid the cries of children and the yelling of a distraught wife. Neighbors respectfully

addressed him as "Signor Emilio," for he was something of a character, one whom everyone generally liked.

Try telling them that Signor Emilio had never traveled outside Italy. He wasn't an adventurous soul, not at all. The farthest he had ever been was to Verona, to challenge a rival journalist to a duel. Otherwise, it was all children and work. Our Salgari was no Jules Verne—he had seen the East only through the pages of atlases. He would spend at least three mornings a week in the local library, reading and taking notes from travel diaries and exotic journals. After which, back home, he would put on his slippers and begin his literary creation: all invented, pure fantasy, distilled with the

sole support of tobacco and a glass of Marsala. He had never been to the Ganges but felt he knew every pebble, and this was what he built his profession on, reinforcing it with certain artistic touches, such as baptizing his children with oriental names: Fatima, Nadir, Omar. The perfect device to make it seem he was a consummate expert on Eastern travels. If they asked him at the restaurant: "But as you've been there, what about Calcutta?" Salgari would stroke his well-groomed mustache and exclaim with the voice of a veteran explorer: "One place in the world looks much the same as another."

Which, indeed, didn't sound too far off the mark. And they'd offer him a drink.

What a shame no one suspected the truth, namely that the great Italian writer of adventure stories preferred to stay at home and to see Malaysia in his own way. But why? Too many insects. Too many diseases. Not to mention monsoons. Travel is tiring and wastes too much valuable time. Signor Emilio did his traveling more comfortably in his armchair, using his imagination, with a healthy amount of added research. No surprise, then, if the odd mistake occasionally crept in—fortresses built of stone instead of bamboo, Mughal ruins described at latitudes the Mughals had never reached, fish unfamiliar to the fishermen of the Brahmaputra. If some academic pointed out the mistake, Salgari would shrug his shoulders: "It's not a university textbook!"

It's hard to disagree: his heroes with such enthralling names were there to bring trepidation to his readers, not to get them through an exam on Hindu civilization. And so, what's the problem if no one is quite certain where Mompracem is? And does it really matter that nobody in Labuan was called Sandokan or Yanez? No, not at all. What mattered was that Salgari's readers wanted to believe it. Not forgetting that Salgari had a family to support, mouths to feed, bills to pay. He had to turn out new books at the rate of one every two months, and with different settings too, from the Antilles to the Siberian steppes, from the Klondike to the Ivory Coast. In short, some margin of error was inevitable, especially when it came to incomprehensible languages, such as Tamil or Dyula, a real problem for someone brought up among the Valpolicella vineyards of the Veneto.

In 1895, Signor Emilio decided to amaze his readers with a new novel set this time in the Antarctic, the queen of continents, still unexplored. A great idea: everyone was talking about the forbidding expanses of ice below Drake Passage, populated by whales and sea monsters. The publisher therefore had high hopes when he read Salgari's manuscript, though he had some serious doubts: "A fascinating book, my dear Emilio, I'm sure. But from a scientific point of view, are you really sure the South Pole can be traversed by bicycle? I've never been there, but don't you think there might be problems with the weather?"

Salgari smiled in his immaculate white suit: "Why do you ask? The expedition in my novel takes every precaution, and the veloc ipedes are of the finest quality."

"I don't doubt it. I fear only that the Antarctic is not the most suitable place for cycling."

Salgari began to show impatience: "It's not exactly a contest, it's a proper exploration. There's a group of tip-top naturalists whose aim is to put up a flag."

"But these tip-top naturalists of yours, excuse me, don't they seem somewhat naïve? Two of them are racing cyclists, chosen for this purpose. There's not a single doctor: no expedition ever leaves without a medical officer. As for the others, they seem a jolly bunch and not much else. Indeed, having run out of gasoline, they have to cross the ice on bicycle, as though it were a Sunday outing. Come on, Emilio, don't you want to give it another look, make a few corrections?"

"Not at all. I'm already on another, about the Caribbean. And what's more, that devil Verne is writing on the Antarctic too."

"Yes, but he does it without bicycles," retorted the publisher.

"All that I've written stands. And you know what? I want bicycles in the title as well. Good day."

Signor Emilio wasn't an easy fellow: he was immovable, and *To the South Pole by Velocipede* was published soon after. His book, it goes without saying, was greeted by the scientific community with a roar of laughter. No one would be so naïve as to move about among the penguins as one might do on a Sunday excursion.

Salgari had gone too far this time: Antarctic expeditions were a costly business, and those who led them were prepared for every danger, taking care over every detail, leaving nothing to chance. This was the reality, far from the ravings of a third-rate writer! And if he really wanted to pursue his idea about the Antarctic, he should at least have waited to study the accounts of the new expedition, that of the Royal Geographical Society, which was about to send its finest men to the South Pole.

And here we reach the point of true interest for our dictionary: we're going to follow what happened not long after, when the *Discovery* sailed in among the icebergs. There was enormous anticipation: the British explorers claimed they had taken care of every detail for what was heralded as the final conquest of the remotest corner of Planet Earth. Three men of the highest caliber—Robert Falcon Scott, Edward Wilson, and Ernest Shackleton—had been chosen to head a vastly expensive expedition, financed by the British government with large private contributions. The *Discovery*'s hold—far from carrying velocipedes—had all that was needed to conquer the Antarctic, from padded tents, to keep out temperatures thirty degrees below zero, to the latest skiing and climbing equipment, and numerous sledges together with packs of dogs. This was science, far more solid than literature. Salgari had to learn that a hostile continent like the South Pole could only be tackled with proper equipment, along with the unrivaled skill of three great explorers. Shackleton and Scott had years of naval experience in the Pacific and Indian oceans, whereas Wilson had graduated in medicine and done much zoological research.

In March 1902, the *Discovery* anchored in front of Ross Ice Shelf, and the three explorers prepared to set off on their mission. They were about to inscribe their names in history. Yes. Even if, to be frank, not everything was proceeding in the best of ways. There had been—one might say—a few hitches, caused perhaps by an excess of enthusiasm. But first things first. Imagine our heroes in dazzling white, surrounded by a multitude of curious penguins.

Scott turned to Shackleton and gave him the order to set up camp with the tents. The Irishman's reply was so extraordinary that I couldn't believe it at first, except that it was all written down in the scientific logs. He gazed at the leader of the expedition and answered: "I really have no idea how tents are put up."

"Sorry?" Scott asked as the temperature began to drop at a rate of four degrees every half hour. Shackleton wasn't the sort to make jokes, nor to beat about the bush, and he confirmed this with an irritating calmness: "I said I don't know how to put up tents. I've never seen them before. It's not my job to set up camp."

Scott spat on the ground—his way of showing embarrassment. This time, to his amazement, he had barely enough time to spit before the saliva had turned to ice. He then turned to Wilson, who managed, however, to get in first: "Don't ask me. I'm the medical officer. I really don't know what tents are."

"So how are we going to sort this out?" Scott asked, hiding himself in his fur hood.

Shackleton didn't lose his usual nonchalance: "We were sure you knew how to put up tents, Robert."

Scott burst into thunderous laughter, which quite alarmed the penguins. "I was sure that in a four-month voyage from England someone would have considered the problem of who would set up camp!" Which led to a heated argument between Scott and Shackleton that was about to degenerate into a fight. For his part, Dr. Wilson was beginning to feel cold and started unpacking the tents in order to save his own life and that of the others. That was the first night the explorers of the *Discovery* spent on the Antarctic ice cap and marked the beginning of an endurance test between three men and their tents. No one knew how to erect them, no one managed to work it out, and however hard they tried, none of them passed a single night without their shelter collapsing on top of them. And that wasn't all: the reports show that neither Scott nor the other two had ever used a sleeping bag, and they all had decided to store up the experience for this trip to Antarctica. Perfect.

At dawn of the second day, as arranged, they prepared to start crossing the ice pack. And there was a further surprise.

This time it was Shackleton who started: "Whose job is it to harness the dogs to the sledges?"

"I've never done it," Scott replied.

"It's not the job of the medical officer," Wilson added, noting that it was beginning to snow heavily.

Shackleton approached the two with a certain impatience: "Do you mean to say that not only can we not put up a tent but none of the three of us can prepare a sledge?"

He received no answer. They were three men lost on the Antarctic ice, in a metaphysical silence. At that moment they found themselves before the cruel and magnificent spectacle of human nature: it is always painful to have to recognize that we are elusive, erratic creatures of irritating incompleteness. What we generally manage to conceal from ourselves explodes at times into something undeniably obvious, and it's a demoralizing experience. There, in those long seconds, we realize how all our mistakes could have been avoided, and how costly our eternal delaying, minimizing, and avoiding becomes each day.

There too, in the case of the sledges, they obviously tried to do the best they could, while the blizzard raged relentlessly. But the results were unsatisfactory, and the dogs—badly harnessed—had to work twice as hard for the whole duration of the expedition. What could be more embarrassing than the realization that you are amateurs on the brink of disaster with no tents and no sledges?

But there was something else.

For the *Discovery* Expedition also entered the history books for other choice details: only on the polar ice cap did Scott, Shackleton, and Wilson realize that none of them had much experience using skis or climbing equipment. If only they'd had bicycles. Yes, they'd have known how to ride them! Perhaps, after all, Salgari's idea about how science could tackle this snow-clad continent had been a real stroke of inspiration. Or rather: Signor Emilio's story, on closer inspection, was even too indulgent, considering that his explorers never ran the risk of dying hungry. The three British explorers, on the other hand, were destined to discover—when it was too late—that their food supplies hadn't been calculated in the best of ways: a trivial arithmetical mistake in the daily rations. What a shame—if only they'd been more careful! But as we know, eager young men are sometimes careless. After all, it was only a brief jaunt to the South Pole, a famously hospitable land. By January 1903 they were on their way home, tired and demoralized, suffering now from scurvy too. You'll say: wasn't one of them a medical officer? He was indeed, but Wilson could hardly be blamed for having underestimated the effects of snow blindness. In short, the other two had to carry him back on their shoulders to the ship.

Rarely have I found such a patent example of amateurishness. But even more remarkable, if this were possible, is the end of the story. Four years later, Ernest Shackleton set sail from England to attempt once more what he had failed to do: to reach the South Pole. As we know, people learn from their mistakes, and future success is built on past errors, on learning from them, on doing better. Shackleton had risked his life during the *Discovery* Expedition, but for this very reason, he set off on this new adventure, perfectly aware of all his shortcomings. He knew there was no room for carelessness or miscalculation: he had already discovered what price was to be paid for thoughtless planning. This was why he chose the *Bjorn*, beyond doubt the most reliable and seaworthy sailing ship.

Certainly. If only it was a little less expensive . . . Shackleton was in a quandary and had to make a choice. He opted for a cheaper solution, sailing instead on a sort of whaling boat from Canada. There we are: it was his choice. This ship, the *Nimrod*, symbolized the whole expedition that followed. Shackleton had set his sights on the ultimate achievement but had to content himself with climbing Mount Erebus, the volcano, because he made exactly the same mistakes he had made six years before. Once again the team had no climbing experience; once again the equipment was inadequate and defective. And whereas on the first occasion everything went wrong with the sled dogs, it was now the turn of Manchurian ponies, which Shackleton had insisted on loading without knowing how to look after them: he found himself with two dozen ponies numb with cold, most of which died after eating salty sand. This was nothing new: the explorers of the *Nimrod* had only to take a closer look at the textbooks. But it was too much to expect of Shackleton. He was voracious, impetuous. Action was all and everything to him. He hated stopping: his idea of life was a continual race, enjoying every moment of excitement. He failed to realize that in this endless contest he had sailed past the finishing posts and was no longer racing to win or for a trophy. Quite simply, he was racing for fear of standing still, as often happens with those whose lives are committed not to winning but to the mere experience of being in the race. The *Nimrod* Expedition, like the *Discovery*, ended at a heavy cost. But evidently, for Shackleton, this was not enough. In 1921, he was ready for another masterpiece of disorganization. This was certainly the most tragic. The ship he chose this time was the *Quest*: never had a boat been less appropriate for a journey to the Antarctic. It was little more than a heap of scrap, impregnated with seal oil and woodwormed to the core.

"This girl can get up to ten knots if you push her," claimed a shifty Danish salesman. Months later Shackleton would discover that she couldn't even manage a speed of six knots, and what was more, she rolled very badly in rough sea. Not insignificant, bearing in mind that Drake Passage is famously the world's stormiest sea passage. But the whole voyage was an ordeal, long before their arrival. The *Quest* was forced to stop at more or less every port for various kinds of repairs, as if to symbolize the spirit of yet another enterprise cobbled together in the passion of the moment, without anyone stopping to think or taking the slightest precautions. They had to lay at anchor in Rio de Janeiro for over a month before setting off again, though none of the crew was ready or keen to continue. And it was there, onboard the *Quest*, that Shackleton died of a heart attack on the night of January 5, 1922. His heart couldn't withstand yet another race, the last of his wild escapades.

> **Questic**—*adjective.* Derived from the Antarctic
> expedition of the *Quest* (1921–1922). *Describes the*
> *condition of someone who sets himself major objectives*
> *in life but does nothing in preparing to achieve them.*
> *A "Questic attitude" is therefore that of someone who*
> *suffers from chronic disorganization, incapable of helping*
> *himself with that minimum of foresight that would make*
> *everything simpler.*

R

Rosabellian

BESS RAHNER HATED THE WAY HER BODY WAS changing. Throughout her life she would remember that day when, at thirteen, in front of the bathroom mirror, she saw one of her long dark hairs drop. At that age, she was told not to worry: it's like a flower in full spring, and if a petal falls it's simply due to a strong gust of wind. But Bess didn't want to admit it. Something inside her was well aware that, as the seasons changed, spring would end, and her black hairs would soon be vulnerable to time. Maybe this was why, from then on, she lived every instant like a slow movement toward her final solstice. Bess, like a child who had spotted the magician's trick, felt she had grasped the humiliating secret of aging, its slow imperceptible slide beneath the skin, until you discover you are different and

have lost your attractiveness. This whole world ignored it except for her. She knew her enemy's tactic. She knew the outcome of the war, that absurd and ultimate law that, sooner or later, would be brought to its armistice through human charter. But she vowed that her resistance would be relentless: from then on, she would constantly check every line on her face, every strand of hair, every glint in that jet-black mop that made her the envy of Brooklyn. Those who loved her hadn't failed to notice the young girl's restlessness. If she felt someone was watching her, she'd begin to fret and rush to the first mirror in search of the first sign of a wrinkle.

"She'll get over it," her parents said, which is how parents dismiss all they find most worrying or don't know how to deal with in their children. "She'll get over it."

Five years later, not only had the obsession not passed but it was becoming more disturbing: Bess was repeating to herself that she would never let herself wrinkle, nor grow fat like Vivian, the red-headed cashier at the local bar, a remnant of past beauty who seemed so piteous that Bess refused to even look at her. She also began to loathe her mother's face, which one day she herself would come to resemble, like an appointment forever feared and postponed. Well, it was then that Bess pictured for the first time—as we might some-times do when our thoughts whirl—a tight, suffocating sheath made of skin and flesh, tight around her to the end of her days. Sometimes the oppressive sensation of this cage woke her at night, or suddenly made her voice crack, just as she was singing "Rosa-belle," her favorite song, on the brightly lit stage on Coney Island. Yes, there was no point in denying it—a desperate urge to escape wracked her until she cried out in pain. But escape from what? How could she break the indestructible chain of nature itself? It was the fall of 1893, and ominous storms brewed over the Atlantic. That was when the two Weisz brothers appeared in her life. They were carried to Bess by the strange current that brings to your island the most fortunate castaways in the whole of the ocean. She saw them for the first time backstage as they were unloading their trunks, and she wasn't too pleased—yet another conjuring act wasn't great news for a place like this, which had been struggling for some time. Everyone thought the boss should be looking for a comedian. A comedian, or at most another couple of dancers. But no, here came these two with their routine, always the same, of disappearing doves and pulling rabbits out of hats. Sure, Bess didn't make the decisions; she was just a singer, and the youngest too, not yet eighteen. And she didn't want to make her problems worse by getting fired. But since she wasn't exactly diplomatic, she went straight to the point: "Did you know the last conjurers who performed here were booed the whole time?" Oddly, neither of the two boys seemed affected or concerned by that head-on attack. They continued unloading their baggage from their creaking cart, with its peeling paint, which wasn't the best of calling cards. Bess returned to the assault: "Because since the girls and I always sing after your act, we'd like to find the audience well disposed. You know how it is—we live on tips. Or does your

society make the wages magically appear at the end of the evening?"
She said this because over the cart, in blue and red, were the words
SOCIETY OF MAGICIANS, probably the most ridiculous name Bess
had ever heard invented for two illusionists. No one picked up the
gauntlet, however. So the girl now became annoyed: "All right, that
means that if, because of you, we're left with no money for supper,
I'll roast one of your doves." And with a smile, Bess headed toward
the dressing room humming the refrain from "Rosabelle," as she did
whenever she came up with some cruel comment that pleased her.
But from behind came a voice with a Hungarian accent: "Do you
imagine these trunks are for doves and gimcracks? They're empty,
Madame Canary."

Quite another feeling stirred in Bess Rahner on hearing herself
called Canary, and yet it made her want to laugh. She thought she
should be angry—or at least pretend to be—but she couldn't help
feeling amused by the name. "And what fine acts might the two of
you be performing with empty trunks?" she said. "Are you going
to close yourselves inside and let the audience guess who you are?"

The reply came from the same magician who had called her
Canary. His name was Theo, but everyone called him Desh. He
was a stocky youth with a nose as pointed as a drill, but what
struck Bess was the geometric arrangement of his hair that no
hurricane would ever have ruffled. He stared at her, and not without a certain pride he evoked the poetic title of the society: "For
your information, we chain ourselves inside the trunks, then give
you the key." Bess held back her laughter, wanting to seem mini-
mally interested: "Impressive. But the Society of Magicians or of
Locksmiths?"

"Let's say it's the Society of Escapers. Right, Erich?"

Erich was Desh's brother, and not one to start chatting up the first canary who happened to pass by. Maybe because he was the real star of the act: in a few hours he'd be risking his life, like every evening, and didn't want to get lost in conversation. So he limited himself to a casual nod and turned away from her, almost disrespectfully, brushing his hands through his hair, which, in stark contrast to that of his brother, was curly and disheveled.

The new arrivals suddenly seemed to Bess like a promising discovery: to get out of a trunk while wrapped in chains appeared such an impossible task that it made her think of her own battle with the shackles of her body. And that evening, as she peeped from behind the curtain to watch the Weisz brothers perform, she already felt a new sense of release, as though she herself were in the chains from which Erich managed so incredibly to break free. There was no doubt: he was indeed a fugitive; he was a source of inspiration; he could escape from any tight spot that would have been fatal for anyone else.

Who knows whether their long love story began that evening on the rickety boards of Coney Island. Bess certainly never felt drawn by the persistent advances of Desh Weisz—his brother was the one who moved her, body and soul, with his wild hair and glaring eyes, beyond which lay a supreme mind, capable of such coolness and concentration that would break open every padlock. She was enraptured more by his prodigious mind than the statuesque physique of a Hungarian Adonis. This was always what she loved in him: to break free, from any cage, from any chain, any restraint. She loved him because the very prison of old age, she thought, might be crushed and defeated by that Hungarian whose fame was growing, each evening, amid public applause while he searched for approval in the restless silence of the eighteen-year-old singer. Yes, for Erich was not indifferent to the darker side of that girl who buried unfathomable moods beneath the notes of "Rosabelle," and indeed it was precisely this shadow that made her appear even more luminous to him. If not immediately, then very soon after.

Desh, for his part, was well aware that his canary was eyeing another nest. He pursued her for some time with bunches of flowers and romantic overtures, after which he accepted the idea that the Society of Magicians wouldn't allow sentimental rivalries. And he stood aside.

Bess Rahner and Erich Weisz married in 1894, and there were plenty of smiles when the celebrant spoke of sacred bonds—before then he had been a man who broke every bond and escaped from every fix. He had recently taken the stage name Houdini, with which he filled the theaters of New York. It was always she who accompanied him onstage: the most trusted of his assistants, who had the most daunting—but most splendid—task of closing the lock, barring the crate, sealing the tank full of water, from which her husband would certainly escape. After all, what is love, if not this guarantee of liberation? What is it, if not this fragile but powerful illusion, such as to make it seem like the only grasp we have on a precarious existence? Bess and Houdini shared everything until the day—October 31, 1926—when he died of peritonitis following a punch to the stomach (he'd agreed to it, to test how strong the muscles of a fifty-year-old were).

It is Houdini's death that interests us most of all in this story. For it relates, more than anything else, to the question of bonds and broken shackles. Human beings live indeed in a state of deep incarceration: we are imprisoned from our birth by the confines of our mortality, which limits our lives, makes them finite. It's no surprise that the first boast of the gods is always their immortality, a condition essential for overcoming the swamp of inhibition. Well, since the beginning of time, humanity has been hoping for something supplementary that could break through this barrier, and could redeem our end under the form of a new beginning—the so-called afterlife. What would it be if not a liberation from the strongest chains we know? Yet Houdini, king escapologist, always firmly and scornfully condemned any display of occultism. And moreover, he was even called by the authorities to unmask the false trickery of necromancers and standard-bearers of the paranormal. He devoted himself to this activity for years. It might seem contradictory: at the evening show he would celebrate the humiliation of chains and padlocks, but during the day he would rail against those who agonized in search of some illusion to break the seal of their last breath.

That night in 1926, however, before he closed his eyes forever at the great threshold, Houdini murmured something to his wife: "For my whole life I've known only how to free myself from shackles, from chains, from trunks, even from coffins. But you know, if there's a way of being free and escaping even death, I'll find that way. Hold a séance each year on the day of my death, and from these words you will know whether I actually come back to meet you." He then added a kind of secret code, the first word of which was *Rosabelle*, a symbol of that old favorite song. After which it was all over.

Bess lit a candle beside the photo of her Erich. And for ten long years she obeyed her husband. She called up his name, without ever getting an answer. On October 31, 1936, the old lady, now perhaps unrecognizable, stared at the lighted candle while her mind was caressed by the bright shadow of a beautiful feeling of relief. Houdini had failed. This time even the great magician had got it wrong; he hadn't managed to escape death like he had escaped from chains. But none of this made her weep, because if even the great Houdini had not humiliated death, then it meant that the time given to us was purely and simply that period of our allotted life, with nothing more after our leap into the darkness. Well, Erich Weisz had spent that whole time with her, he had chosen to spend it with her. I like to think that Bess suddenly saw everything clearly. She had experienced the great contradiction of love, which offers you the most sublime escape from reality together with its perfect opposite—it's the only reality from which you don't have to feel the need to escape. This is why Mrs. Weisz, on that Halloween of 1936, before blowing out the candle for the last time, spoke what was perhaps the most beautiful declaration of love. She simply said: "Good night, Erich."

And there was a sweet darkness.

> **Rosabellian**—*adjective.* Derived from the favorite song
> of W. Beatrice Rahner, known as Bess (1876–1943).
> *Indicates a deep and extraordinary feeling between*
> *two human beings, for which all that belongs to the*
> *experience of love is not enough. In this case there is a full*
> *consecration to the other of all that is most precious to us:*
> *our time on Earth.*

Shenshinism

C AN ANYONE TOIL AWAY WRITING FOR THEIR whole life and then pass into history for a brawl that happened at their house, at their table, between two other writers? Yes, sadly it's possible. But it's even sadder when the writer in question had no shortage of talent, and indeed was admired by Russian literati as one of their finest writers, from whom they drew inspiration and guidance. And yet the name Afanasy Afanasyevich Fet will probably mean nothing to you. But if you were to mention his name in Moscow, you would most likely hear the response: "Ah, of course, the one who invited Tolstoy and Turgenev for lunch, when the two of them almost came to blows in the sitting room." That's all. Nothing else about Fet. No one recites his poetry from memory; no one has ever turned his surname into an adjective to describe any poetic style.

That's right, though Fet remains a great poet all the same.

Except that he is cruelly portrayed as a man constantly out of time. And I think his story is worth including in our dictionary for this very reason. At every key point in his life, Fet arrived either too early or too late, continually failing to catch the right moment. Then again, how often have we had to reflect upon the crucial importance of a moment? Our lives move in sudden directions through chance, frequently dependent on minuscule shifts of time: "If I had managed to catch that train," "If I hadn't missed that meeting," "If I had answered that phone call," "If I hadn't stopped outside the door and overheard that conversation," and so forth. It all depends on fragments of a second, and on apparently irrelevant details that make the difference: some advanced form of science is needed to synchronize the film of our lives with the soundtrack of time, its events, its opportunities. Well, Afanasy Fet was a disaster in this respect. While many of us have our highs and lows in the eternal run-up to the golden moment, he never even managed to get halfway. By which I mean: the surfer who rides the wave may end up in the water, he might miss the flow of the tide or the wind, but he can always get back up.

Just so we're clear, before returning to Fet, think for example how Richard Nixon succeeded—or didn't—in grasping the moment. In September 1952 he astonished his fellow Americans with one of the most vibrant television appearances in US history. Though not yet forty, he was the Republican vice presidential candidate, except that a press probe had made allegations of improper campaign fundraising that could affect the outcome of the election itself. Well, the year 1952 was still prehistoric, compared with the electoral hullabaloo of today, all built around window dressing and comic timing. Politics, the sublime art of rhetoric, was proudly

dismissive of television, happy to leave it as musical entertainment and quiz shows for housewives. This is why it caused such astonishment that Nixon should appear on television screens from Texas to Maine to defend himself so staunchly against the allegations. Oh, that day he certainly knew how to ride the wave—not like Afanasy! For, apart from those who were outraged by his unseemly electioneering among dancing girls and Jerry Lewis, it was clear all the same that the bold Californian had everything to gain from appearing in millions of homes, trailers, and diners to declare his innocence. Proved by the fact that the Republicans won the election a few months later with a convincing majority of more than seven million votes. Which all goes to show that Nixon was anything but a novice when it came to communication. During his term in office, as further proof, he took part in the so-called Kitchen Debate, another milestone in the history of television politics. And here too everything was determined by a question of seconds on the occasion of Nixon's visit to a great exhibition of American products in no less a place than Moscow in the forlorn hope of a dialogue between the two superpowers. It just so happened that at the same moment the Soviet entourage was entering the building with First Secretary Nikita Khrushchev, whose planned route, however, was a safe distance from Nixon's. Heaven forbid that they should meet: the future of the planet was at risk, on the brink of nuclear catastrophe. But meanwhile there was a few minutes' delay, a small organizational hitch concerning those entering and leaving a stand displaying electrical kitchen appliances. Nixon and Khrushchev, to the horror of their staff, found themselves next to each other, among dishwashers, blenders, and toasters. Life was offering Nixon another opportunity: could he make the most of it? The answer was yes, and that parade of cooking pots provided an unforgettable backdrop. Amid vitriolic barbs and mutual fake praise, the USSR and the United States amazingly looked each other in the eye, for the first time, without averting their gazes, with that sly fox Nixon, who seized the opportunity to heap praise on American consumerism, from Pepsi to discount supermarkets and canned food. Talk about the good surfer. Here, once again, he created a media sensation, so that the historic meeting was recorded in color and broadcast with this futuristic format on television. In short, Nixon had already made himself the pioneer of a new cathodic politics, all entrusted to aerials and remote controls. And against this background, a year later, he stood as Eisenhower's successor for the White House.

Unfortunately, however, the wind can often ruffle the waves in an instant. Against him the Democrats fielded a young senator from Massachusetts, one John Fitzgerald Kennedy, who seemed easily beatable. The hero of the Kitchen Debate was an experienced salesman, and vice president to boot. And so? For once the favorite Richard Nixon dramatically resembled Afanasy Fet—the trophy slipped from his hands just as he was savoring the sure prospect of victory. It happened in the fall of 1960, when the first television electoral duel was staged (or rather, broadcast). Poor Nixon came out badly. He wasn't helped by turning up in an ugly brown jacket and slightly unshaven, refusing—goodness knows why—to wear the minimum of makeup. To complete the picture, he was dosed up with antihistamines after a minor operation. Verdict? Nixon signed his own death warrant. Not in ink, but in sweat. Midway through the debate, the camera caught—by chance, here too—a telltale droplet that trickled down, down, down his face to his chin. And since television is unforgiving, the conclusion was unanimous. Kennedy smiled calmly under his dashing forelock, while

Nixon sweated nervously like a schoolkid who hadn't studied for his geography exam. Kennedy was the overwhelming winner— and not just of the evening but of the election too.

Skeptics will say: come on, it doesn't take just a drop of sweat to decide who gets to the White House. Well—as you're about to hear—all it took was one spark to deprive Afanasy Fet of his great love. And this was just one of the countless chance events that studded his life of lost opportunities.

So to begin with, put yourself in his position, and be prepared for the worst, because his misfortunes started very early. And not because he was struck by some terrible disaster but through the fact that he was promptly deprived of everything that other people can typically feel sure about.

One thing at a time.

What can we feel more sure about than our name? Generally speaking, every John Smith might think that whatever he might be deprived of in life, he won't lose the right to call himself Smith. Well, not necessarily.

Afanasy Fet, for example, at the age of thirteen, imagined that his surname for the whole of his life would be Shenshin. It was just a name, you'll say. Well, no, it was much more. Our fine young boy was the son of a nobleman, and like all children of high birth, he felt entitled to look forward to a future of social respect and prosperity. This had been so for Tolstoy, for Pushkin, and later for Dostoevsky. But for young Afanasy Shenshin, fate decreed that such opportunities would sooner or later slip away.

In 1835, he and his parents were summoned to a government office. Reason? Investigations.

And all three turned up.

It was like receiving a sentence of life imprisonment. Because the official, after much hesitation, had to explain that there was a problem: theirs was not a legal family. But why not? How could an ordinary Russian family suddenly not be legal?

The official opened a file at least two inches thick. On careful investigation it had emerged that the marriage was not valid. Afanasy's father banged his fist on the desk, attracting the attention of two other clerks. Such madness was unconscionable; he and his wife had simply been married abroad. Yes, of course, but . . . The official put on his spectacles and produced another file with another particular. Apart from the marriage itself, the disturbing aspect was that . . . in a word . . . How can one put it? . . . To be brief, the little boy was no longer his father's son. This has to be a joke! Unfortunately not. No documentary proof. End of surname Shenshin.

Now, in retrospect we might say it was a stupid bureaucratic detail, the obtuse nit-picking of provincial officials. The whole thing, by their own admission, was somewhat ridiculous. But it had a most unfortunate consequence: until the matter was resolved, Afanasy lost all entitlements and privileges. Just imagine the scene—his mother in tears, his father with his hands in his hair, while thirteen-year-old Afanasy was trying to work out exactly what the trouble was. No one wanted to explain it to him. Neither the official nor the clerks had the heart to tell him that, in Russia at that time, having no noble title was a guarantee of all kinds of trouble—he couldn't study beyond a certain level, couldn't join clubs or mix with young ladies of noble birth, would have to forego everything that the likes of Tolstoy and Turgenev could do. Before they left, however, the official tried to reassure them: it would be enough to make an application and wait for the outcome. And indeed, the documents were duly signed, sealed, and dispatched. Do you know how long it took to complete the process of petitions and appeals that enabled Afanasy to regain his titles and surname? Forty-one years. And meanwhile he had to be satisfied with Fet, his mother's surname.

Didn't I say that his whole story was one of bad timing and lost opportunities? But this was just the first in a long series of events.

In 1845, Fet joined the cavalry and went off to war. He said goodbye to Maria Lewich, the Polish girl he so dearly loved, and swore that he would never, but never, have left for the front had it not been for the war in Crimea, a chance not to be missed. And his assessment was not altogether wrong, for on the field of battle, through military promotion, he could regain the status that bureaucrats had taken from him. Perfect. Maria accepted this, and prayed for him each day: not only that he might be kept safe but also that the heavens would at last restore his honor.

This—in theory, let us say—was what the rules then provided: a noncommissioned officer like Afanasy would receive a noble title upon gaining two medals with a corresponding promotion in rank. That year Crimea witnessed no more tireless a soldier. It was his appointment with destiny, and Fet had no intention of letting it slip by.

Three months later, at last, his beloved Maria received a letter from the front. Their prayers had been answered; he could now boast two medals on his breast and a glittering officer's uniform. He had done it! Hallelujah.

And indeed, with a great smile painted on his face, the new officer Afanasy Fet appeared with his bravery medal before the general to receive his colors.

The general smiled back. Didn't he know that the rules had

been redrafted just a week before? The title now was only to be won with four medals and a double promotion in rank. Afanasy cursed his cruel fate, and wrote to Maria that she was not to stop her religious effort but, if anything, should double it. After which he took his courage in both hands and threw himself once again, body and soul, into the cauldron of the Crimea. Could he ever renounce what was due to him?

At the end of spring Maria received news from the field hospital: the goal had been reached, but at an enormous price. As soon as he could stand up, Afanasy dragged himself straight before the general: despite his bandages and his limp, on his chest he had the four requisite medals, together with a splendid lieutenant's uniform.

The general didn't know what to say: the tsar had been counseled to raise the criteria once again, so that seven medals were needed and the rank of regimental leader.

It seems incredible, but this is the story of Afanasy Fet's life.

At which point he'd had enough—at the age of nearly thirty he concluded that life was against him and the whole of humanity seemed to be enjoying the pleasures of Eden at his expense. For what devil of a reason was his road full of curves and steep climbs, while for others it was all a smooth ride? Where had he gone wrong? Why did his stove always have to be cold and the wood damp in the middle of a snowstorm? It was 1850 when Afanasy returned to the arms of Maria Lewich exactly the same as he had left her years before, namely with no money, no title, and no official father.

He could hardly imagine that Maria meanwhile had also slipped through his fingers. Not through sickness, which would at least have been more bearable. No, once again, chance had been at work, snatching from him the woman he loved. Maria Lewich had burned to death in her bed, from the spark of a lantern that had set fire to the straw.

He lived out the rest of his days in a mix of anger and desperation. Some mysterious law seemed determined to deprive him of whatever he attempted, while displaying around him the calm radiance of happy families and adoring couples.

In the chill November of 1892, Afanasy was a decrepit poet of seventy, surrounded by other men of letters, all more famous and celebrated than he, however much they privately praised him as their guide and their inspiration. But the affliction of that life of constant disillusion had made him a bitter man and consumed him from within. He knew, he felt with agonizing clarity, that he had tried in every way to make the most of life, but it was life itself that had eluded him. Because, yes, there are some who choose not to live their lives to the full, but there are also certain lives that refuse to be lived, that slip out of your hands. On the evening of November 21, Afanasy shut himself in his room, took a knife, and tried to kill himself. He didn't succeed. The blade wasn't sharp enough, so the wounds were minor. And—who knows—it seems his choice of the wrong knife was perhaps a sign, for once, that chance was on his side, to keep him alive. But no, while the knife had failed to kill him, a few moments later he had a heart attack.

And so ended the terrible life of Afanasy Fet, who was, in effect, prevented from existing.

I don't know whether this might be the deep secret of his poetry, which I made myself read at all costs, even though—it goes without saying—he is one of the so-called lesser authors, at whose name booksellers and librarians ask: "Sorry, who?"

"Afanasy Fet: the greatest Russian poet." This, at least, is how it seems to me.

> **Shenshinism**—*noun.* Derived from Afanasy
> Afanasyevich Fet-Shenshin (1820–1892). *Indicates the*
> *state of mind of those who feel every opportunity in their*
> *life slips through their hands and they cannot hold on to*
> *what others are freely given. Shenshinism is therefore that*
> *immense difficulty you experience in something that for*
> *everyone else is simple.*

Tautonaic
and Telegramic

A SIXTY-MINUTE JOURNEY ISN'T SHORT; NOR IS it particularly long. It depends where you're going. Many major cities are linked by high-speed trains that take around an hour, and you can fly hundreds of miles in the same time. During the journey, you can read, sleep, eat, check your watch every so often to see how much of the sixty minutes is left.

Fine, but I challenge anyone to imagine such a journey in an elevator. Yes, the poky cabin already invented by Archimedes three centuries before Christ, which makes claustrophobics anxious even for those few minutes between ground and roof. One hour. That's how long it takes to reach the deepest extraction level in the TauTona gold mine in South Africa, almost two and a half miles down. No one in the world works any lower. And we can almost imagine listening to the conversations between those thousands of miners who, to reach their workplace each day, after their bus and train journeys, have to add a further sixty minutes' descent into hell: "Did you see the match with the Kaizer Chiefs on TV last night?" "Oh yes, we can talk about it in the elevator on the way back up," and so forth. Not far from Johannesburg, the mine is like a long straw that sucks gold from the belly of the earth, and it's no coincidence that the whole province is called Gauteng, which in the Sotho-Tswana languages means "place of gold." Tons and tons of gold are extracted every year, at massively high risk and with many deaths, down there, deep down, where the smallest air-conditioning failure would send the thermometer shooting up to oven temperatures. But this, as we know, is the price of gold.

It's curious how humanity, since the earliest times, has pursued the king of metals as a symbol of light and divinity. When Moses encounters the Lord on Mount Sinai, he receives the order to cover the women of the Chosen People with gold ornaments and, like Midas, to fashion articles for temple worship. Not to mention the famous three magi at Bethlehem—didn't they bring gold, incense, and myrrh to glorify the god incarnate? This is no surprise: the shiny metal contains in it the secret of life, the power of the sun that animates and nourishes everything. It is no coincidence that in dozens of languages the ideogram for the sun is the same as that for gold, as if to say this chemical element contains within it the same essence that makes the planet fertile, and humanity with it. So men dig down into the spectral depths of TauTona to snatch fragments of light from the earth. It's a glaring contradiction: the sun crosses the sky, but its metallic counterpart lies buried thousands of feet beneath our feet, in a place that will

never, ever be reached by a ray of natural light. In short, to enjoy a slice of heaven, the AngloAmerican corporation had to dig a tunnel into hell.

My reason for talking about this emblematic case of TauTona is because it has often made me think how clumsy and strange human machinations are. We aim toward a certain objective, we make it the very horizon of our every action and thought, without realizing that the path for obtaining it will take us far away, in the exact opposite direction. It's a detestable implication of our much-vaunted strength of will: to get hold of what we have set our minds on, we are prepared to suspend all clear judgment over how we get it, and its consequences. I repeat: at TauTona, in order to obtain shiny luminous gold for humanity, 5,600 miners are sent down into a maze of tunnels where the sun is an abstract concept. The negation of light to possess the light. How much of us there is in the absurdity of that mine—the basest actions perpetrated in the name of affection and love, the cruelest wars fought for peace, death sown everywhere for the protection of life, poverty disguised as an instrument for well-being. I fear we are all down there, an hour by elevator below sea level, all busily digging like moles in search of an absolute opposite.

There's a remarkable stubbornness in all of this, a sort of temporary narcosis, to which on reawakening we will find a cruel reckoning, rather like the German foreign secretary Arthur Zimmermann during World War I. I find his case paradoxical, distinguished as it is by the typical mixture of culpable incapacity and naïve stupidity that marks us out in the most critical moments. But let's start at the beginning.

In 1916, the world was literally in flames. War raged in every part, from the Balkans to Baghdad, from the Caucasus to Palestine.

Only Russia, once it had become Bolshevik under Lenin, would eventually pull out of the slaughter, withdrawing inside its borders. The *Kaiserreich* of Wilhelm II had alliances with the Ottoman Turks and the old Habsburg Empire, but its only hope was that the United States of America would keep its promise to remain neutral. This had been the case so far. Fortunately, despite the sinking of great ships like the *Lusitania* by German submarines, there had been no signal from Washington that it wanted to enter the arena. Excellent. Otherwise, there could be very serious trouble. So Berlin kept its fingers crossed.

And it would have been better for it to have done no more.

But since government ministries generally tend to go further than crossing their fingers, someone advised the chancellor to put foreign affairs in the hands of a fine strategist, a shrewd diplomat, a smart thinker who'd know best how to deal with the Americans, nipping any argument in the bud and ensuring they hadn't the slightest reason to enter the war. And who should be given such an appointment? Who should deal with such a delicate matter, all the more delicate since Kaiser Wilhelm II with the charm of a pachyderm was piling one insult on another with his gaffes and his vitriolic outbursts? The decision on whom to appoint fell to the chancellor. Theobald von Bethmann-Hollweg—Lord help us—was the most indecisive and hesitant man imaginable, one of those who never takes a step forward without taking at least four back and two sideways, just so that nobody could say he hadn't tried everything. And since His Imperial and Royal Majesty had a disagreeable character and his excesses had to be rectified daily, the chancellor tended to surround himself with figures as cautious and unassuming as possible. Even better if they were introverted and had little to say: the last thing he wanted was cantankerous ministers in addition to the emperor. And so the choice fell on Arthur Zimmermann, who, to judge from his character, wouldn't cause any problems. The new foreign secretary—a key role during a world war—would be this unlikely fifty-year-old, hidden behind the slender body of a sixteen-year-old that had not been shaped in the gymnasium of life, with a look always of such bewilderment, and skin so white and smooth that it looked like the Polish porcelain typical of the town where he was born in the northeast, a town that much later would be renamed Treuburg, "Loyal Town." Arthur himself was loyal, perhaps too loyal: loyal to everyone, loyal to a fault, with that dubious and extreme form of loyalty that strays into the more subservient kind of acquiescence, to the extent of never wishing to make enemies. For the last ten years Zimmermann had therefore been the quintessence of Prussian sentimentality, proving himself to be more an institutional butler, a political coachman, one of those master gardeners with smooth hands that delegate the pruning of the bushes to others, keeping only the rose beds for their own velvet touch. Zimmermann was proud of it. Never once in so many years had he raised his voice inside the stucco walls of the palace, and he was pleased to be a servant of the *Kaiserreich*, by which he meant one of those who, for reasons of state, always nod and smile, showing their disagreement with a less enthusiastic nod or a wince of a smile. And so while the guns blasted, it was he who was chosen, loyal Arthur, one who maybe thought *artillery* itself was just another kind of art. There it is. Since his task was to keep the Americans out of the fray, perhaps his meekness would turn out to be the right medicine. And with this hope in everyone's hearts, Zimmermann swore in his role as foreign secretary to work for the good of the Reich.

It must be said that he tried his best.

He reassured the US president in every way, wrote encouraging letters, and smiled as he shook ambassadors' hands. His was a difficult tightrope to walk, considering that German submarines meanwhile had orders to attack any US ship that appeared to be carrying supplies to Germany's enemy powers in Europe. At first It really seemed as if this approach was working; maybe the distinguished Polish butler from Loyal Town had clearly in mind how to work for the good of the German people. But then?

Then the day came.

When Zimmermann inexplicably attached his name to one of the most mind-boggling stupidities in twentieth-century history.

You know how, in certain arguments between people who know each other, everyone's perfectly aware that the mere mention of a particular subject is like pouring a can of gasoline on a fire? Perfect. Well, for Woodrow Wilson, the US president, that taboo subject was Mexico. It was understandable. He had been humiliated a few months earlier—in front of his electorate and the whole world—by a kind of hotheaded Mexican bandit called Pancho Villa, who had dared to cause havoc in New Mexico. Those were the years in which Pancho was challenging the United States, and now he had gone too far. So Wilson had decided to make him pay the price, sending to the remote border town of Columbus a gigantic army of tanks and armored cars as had never been seen before, complete even with air cover that was revolutionary at the time. This vast force was led by none other than General Pershing, and with him George Patton, who would pass into history as a US Army man of steel. Well, after months of siege, Pershing and Patton went back home with their tails between their legs because the so-called Centaur of the North had managed this time to get away, making fools of that whole military deployment, compared to whom Achilles and Agamemnon were amateurs. In short? That devil of a Centaur had made a laughingstock of America, and Wilson boiled with rage each time anyone even accidentally mentioned Mexico.

Cleverly, the German foreign secretary Zimmermann did even worse.

The whole of Europe well knew, in the midst of war, that telegram transmissions were intercepted by the British navy, which had always been at the forefront when it came to deciphering coded messages. But Zimmermann seemed naïvely unaware of this. Or maybe he wanted at all costs to fathom the worst to get to the best, just as one searches for gold in the bowels of the earth. People often talk about the greatness of human genius. Here I am describing the greatness of human error, which is sometimes all the more incredible when it seems more subtly intentional. And there it is. On January 16, 1917—just as President Wilson was being roundly mocked by Pancho Villa—the minister sent a telegram from Berlin, addressed to Mexico City. Writing to the German ambassador, Zimmermann stated that his prime objective was peace with the United States, but . . . but he added that in the event of a US entry into the war, Germany then offered Mexico a military alliance against Washington, for a just war in which the Mexicans would finally reconquer a swathe of territories, from Texas to Arizona.

Political suicide?

Suffice it to say that its author deserved his nickname Telegram Zimmermann.

It was a catastrophic error. Great Britain immediately intercepted the message, decoded it in an instant, and was very happy to rouse President Wilson against the Germans. Meanwhile even Mexico preferred to distance itself from Berlin, declining the minister's kind offer. A complete debacle.

But how complex and unfathomable is the human mind! It's as if sometimes the descent into the inferno of our misdeeds is not enough to satisfy us: we need to go further, and to tell ourselves that we are illiterate novices in life, we feel an irrepressible need to plumb the depths in order to investigate if not the peaks then at least the troughs of our reactivity. It almost seems that in the persistent pursuit of error we find the strongest instinct of the human beast, that which makes it desperately demand some tangible sign of its own existence as a living creature. And what happens if we search for this extreme sense of life in the depth of rebellion, in the drastic and totalizing experience of derailment? There is always something magnificent about devastation: however dramatic, it is riveting to experience for those who witness it. And this is sometimes enough to create a monstrous appetite for destruction: it's a tremor of pure life, and from some unfamiliar place it finally speaks to us, of our strengths and our limitations.

This is what happened in Berlin: Arthur Zimmermann—for the good of the German people—took the elevator down even deeper than the bowels of TauTona. He had made a mistake, but even more disastrous was the deluge that it caused. You'll be amazed to hear that as soon as the whole world shouted conspiracy, thinking unanimously that the German chancellery couldn't possibly have slipped up so spectacularly, Zimmermann didn't heave a sigh of relief or quietly rejoice that peril had been averted; he called a press conference, and before the startled eyes of those present, he took all the blame for the fateful telegram. So it was true? Had Germany really proposed an improbable alliance against the United States to Mexico's Pancho Villa?

Yes, yes, all true.

Dozens of German diplomats hurried to correct him: there had been a misunderstanding; without doubt, the *Kaiserreich* certainly didn't intend to provoke the United States. But Zimmermann didn't back down in the slightest—the telegram was genuine. And a few months later President Wilson announced the United States' entry into the war.

Barely three months went by before the German government was already in difficulty, badly rocked by the scandal the telegram had caused, and Zimmermann in November 1917 was forced to leave the ministry. Heavily defeated in war, Germany would change forever, while the United States, as a direct result of its triumphant involvement in the conflict, at last claimed its position as a world power. In short, if the whole world was indelibly altered, it was thanks to a crazy, incomprehensible telegram. It was thanks to a series of errors by a sober, ingenuous foreign secretary who was convinced he was pursuing only the highest good for the German people.

Zimmermann had been seeking the sunlight reflected in gold. Who knows whether he looked back to consider what he had done. He would have seen only the pitch darkness of TauTona, an hour's elevator ride from the surface of the earth.

> **Tautonaic**—*adjective.* Derived from the TauTona gold mine in South Africa. *Indicates the obsessive search for something good, so dazzling that it leads you to waste your life doing the exact opposite. And so "a Tautonaic choice" is something that, though it is done in pursuit of*

a theoretical good, leads to a drastic deterioration in a person's daily life.

Telegramic—*adjective.* Derived from the nickname given to Arthur Zimmermann (1864–1940), German foreign secretary. *Indicates a chain of actions begun with the best of intentions that later reveals itself to be an infernal round of disastrous errors leading to exactly the opposite result. Consequently, the term telegramic includes everything that relates to inept, clumsy, and deleterious decisions taken in pursuit of one's own good. And it can be used as an adjectival noun ("never seen a telegramic like me") to mean one of life's novices whose actions have slid dramatically out of control.*

U

Unloyalism

LOCKED UP IN THE ASPHYXIATING DARKNESS OF the cattle wagon, Nellie tried desperately to at least recognize the noises outside. The human senses tend to display a certain solidarity, so that our hearing immediately compensates for poor eyesight in a unity that we might describe as tender and moving, if it were not that our awareness of reality is above all defensive, and therefore climactic.

Her journey had started several hours earlier, and the wagon would soon be arriving at Blackwell's Island. Nellie already seemed to hear the splashing of water around her, mixed with the laughter of those escorting her. And she had the impression that the whole outside world was no longer for them, like a garden whose gate is slammed in the face of children who would like to play there. After all, that was how it was: the garden of reality wasn't open to everyone—to enter it you always needed someone who would stand surety for you. Otherwise? Otherwise there was Blackwell's Island.

There must have been ten of them, bound at their wrists and thrown in, one against the other, so tightly they couldn't even move. One girl, perhaps the youngest, had fallen as she'd climbed in, cutting her knee on the rusty metal step. Yet she didn't complain. Before the barred door was bolted with two turns of the lock, Nellie had seen her smile, guileless and terrible, licking the fresh blood from her fingers. Another girl, whose crying sometimes sounded like hysterical laughter, refused to sit on the two parallel benches and stretched her legs out to occupy the whole space of the wagon. Her sweaty body had regressed to its purely biological state and shamelessly exposed her disheveled mass of thighs and breasts to lose all the innate charm the female body already extols by the age of ten as a temple of mysterious secrecy. Here, on the road for Blackwell's Island, the temple of Venus had become a butchery.

Nellie strove to memorize every image, as one might do with paintings in a museum where studying pictures is tantamount to squeezing out some vague concept of art. In this case, the descent into the inferno of madness would reveal the precariousness of her mental balance, and how slippery the crest of normality is. Who were these women of occasional charm, not without a certain austere nobility yet treated like animals and packed into a hospital wagon? The certificates described Blackwell's Island as an asylum for lunatics: lunacy, affected by the moon, and Nellie couldn't

help thinking that the moon moves the tides, making pregnant wives give birth, to the delight of husbands who are so proud at having married before God a childbearing woman, a good house-wife, and a fervent Christian. Yet before her she saw an assortment of discordant notes, of creatures off the rails, to whom the moon had not ordained a glorious birth but the abortion of a lost mind. Perhaps it was because the blond-haired skeleton that happened to be beside her was continually repeating the same monosyllable, in an almost musical tone that Nellie thought was something like an old Mexican lullaby she had learned while she was working across the border. And the intermittent sweetness of that melody was so poignant that she found it impossible to listen, perhaps because it ill-concealed the abyss of a perverse solitude, something that is never, ever allowed in a woman. Meanwhile the loud squeaking of an entrance door announced, like the blast of a bugle, that they had entered the institution. The rattling of the wheels beneath their feet at last stopped, and there was a long silence. This is how Blackwell's Island greeted her: with the silence of a cathedral, when you think that even to swallow will sound blasphemous, costing you dear in contrition and penitence. And so as not to break the tomb-like silence, you stop living, hold your breath, hope to vanish, cursing yourself for having a naturally noisy body. Nellie held her breath; even the air didn't fully belong to her, and she felt duty bound not to abuse it.

Then suddenly it happened—the lock creaked as though it had been closed since time immemorial, and the door opened. Their eyes were flooded with a milky light, tinged with an acrid smell of bleach. Wasn't it, after all, the place for cleansing foul minds? Weren't they trying to wipe out the stains of a twisted psyche, scrubbing away memories and phobias with sodium hypochlorite? So be it. The most difficult ten days of her life were about to begin.

No journalist like Nellie Bly had ever passed through the gates of Blackwell's Island. In 1887, she was twenty-three, and when Joseph Pulitzer, the brilliant editor of *New York World*, asked whether she would do an investigation into the women's asylum, he never imagined she would reply "Sure, I'll have myself committed."

Pulitzer ran his hand through his thick dark beard as if almost to check the lines of his face. He always did this when humanity amazed or terrified him, experiences that in this case had somewhat merged. What concerned him now was his own inability to work people out: Elizabeth Cochran, pen name Nellie Bly, seemed like one of those daughters of prosperous families who dressed in secondhand clothing to flaunt their independence from the parental purse. He had never expected much from this kind of Aphrodite who was so accustomed to the enameled drawing room fireplace that she would never want to dirty herself at a coal stove. And journalism—for Pulitzer, at least—always meant delving into the underbelly of modern society.

But this delicate-faced twenty-three-year-old had taken him by surprise, adding as she moved toward the door: "It doesn't require much to be taken for a lunatic: come and fetch me after ten days."

"I hope in ten days they won't have trepanned your head," Pulitzer said, putting it down to an excess of youthful enthusiasm.

"If they trepan my head, then you'll have plenty to report. Bye." And she vanished with a faintly ridiculous hat on her head.

And so began the first undercover assignment in the history of journalism. Nellie Bly spent a week and a half among hysterical and psychotic women, observing humiliations, violence, assaults, and all that can transform a would-be hospital into a Dantean circle of hell. Yet what is most astonishing when we read this reporter's daring account (which then became a book) is Nellie's surprise in exploring her own madness. Sure—it's true—her madness was playacting. But how simple it was to pass herself off credibly as being different, alien, irrational. In doing so, Nellie Bly had used her other side, that hidden and unexplored side, the one each of us suppresses because it would clash with that identity we keep under close guard. This is what amazes me about the brave story of her stay on Blackwell's Island. For ten long days Nellie easily managed to make herself seem mad, but in reality she was one of us, a person who could be described as sane and with functional mental balance, an individual in control of her senses who had no difficulty answering the question "Who are you?" This is the heart of the problem: do we know how to answer this question? As lucid and normal people, do we really hold the key to our own identity? Do we keep hold of our own reins? Nellie's case tells us that the room in which madness—or, if you prefer, disorientation—lives always communicates with that of perfect sense, and the door between the two rooms is always open. We find it reassuring at our peak of intellectual vigor that we can tell ourselves this, but at the same time we quake with fear at the first crack in this marble solidity. In short, take everything away from me, but not the knowledge of who I am.

And yet there is someone who, without ending up at Blackwell's Island, managed to spend his whole life playing with the crucial question of "Who am I?" In my view it's an incredible story that revolves around a photograph dating from the early 1930s, taken among rowing trophies in a corridor at Cambridge. But let us first move one step back.

Donald Duart Maclean was born in May 1913 in a smart house in Marylebone, central London, among neatly clipped hedges and windows polished like mirrors. His father, Sir Donald Maclean, was a powerful political figure, one of those who were greeted in the street by a chauffeur holding open the rear door of a limousine shinier even than the windows. Well, young Donald grew up with all that could turn him into a bright young member of the new London establishment: top preparatory schools, boarding schools, and a scholarship to Cambridge. Here he is, therefore, in 1931, photographed in pullover and tie, hair neatly groomed, with four college friends, the inseparable John, Kim, Guy, and Anthony: identical smiles, identical pullovers, identical expressions. Someone who knows that one day in the future he will show this photo to his grandchildren, and they too will be sent to the same college and will wear the same pullover. Guy was the son of a naval commander; Kim was the son of a senior diplomatic advisor to the king of Arabia. In that photo there is England's elite, England's investment in the future. And as in the eternal cycle of the seasons, all was proceeding as expected, in the sense that Donald and his companions were setting off to become no less than what everyone expected: their identity lay waiting for them as an appointment crystallized in time, a bespoke suit that the finest tailors had been cutting for them ever since the day they were born. For I fear it is true that we are born a second time, when we reach our early twenties after a long gestation period. Around those five young men in the photo there's an invisible obstetrical department that is preparing them each day to match up to everyone's expectations. And it is a second birth in every respect, more painful because it is we alone who force ourselves toward the light, without being pushed out by a mother's contractions.

In the case of Donald Duart Maclean, then, everything was so predictable as to seem tedious. As the son of a knight, he would become a man of power, a leading politician, one of those whose secretary would hold his umbrella for the ten paces between the car and his country cottage. All written. All arranged. The umbrella, the car, and the cottage, there waiting for him.

But was it so?

Or maybe you're waiting for his sudden conversion into a street rebel, a sworn enemy of family conventions?

It will disappoint you to know that nothing of the kind took place. Much worse. Or, if you like, much more inspired. Because his second birth was an apparent triumph: by the mid-1930s young Donald was already a smart-suited official at the Foreign Office and was given diplomatic assignments of the greatest delicacy at the British embassies in Paris and Washington. For more than ten years he was all that he was supposed to be: rich, respectable, and respected. It's just a shame about one defect that prostrated him too many times, alas, before the god of Alcohol; during his nights of bingeing in the US capital it started to be rumored that Mr. Maclean drank so much that he rambled and became delirious. He was heard shouting in the middle of the night that he was an undercover agent for the Soviet secret service, and that he reported each day to Moscow. No one, of course, gave any weight to such whiskey-sodden deliria, nor did they dream of reserving a cell for him on any Blackwell's Island. However hopeless and woebegone, the identity of a thoroughbred horse like Donald was not in question, nor was it for any of the four young aristocrats with whom he had sat his exams for Trinity Hall or the rowing champions among the college blues. The five young men in the grainy photograph, apart from their pullovers, had this in common: their pedigree. It would protect them throughout their lives from any attack on the fortress of "Who am I?" and they could even shout from the rooftops that they were communist spies and no one would raise any questions. Wrongly.

Because alcohol brought out the truth in Donald Maclean. For over ten years he had a totally double identity—he was an austere British diplomat as well as a faithful communist under orders from Stalin. And he wasn't the only one. All five of those students in pullovers lived lives above suspicion, with one foot in London and the other in the Kremlin. The double life of Anthony Blunt went on for thirty years, during which everyone still looked upon him as an eminent art historian, while Kim Philby even managed to be appointed—with no shadow of suspicion—as head of British counterintelligence.

But of the five friends in the photograph, the one I am most struck by is Donald Maclean, the only one who, in his alcoholic carousing, veered dangerously out from under his cover. He, the son of an overweening father, didn't know how, in the end, to balance the incredible blood oath sealed in some Cambridge bedroom with an inviolable commitment to life. He was in fact the first to give himself away and had to escape to the Soviet Union. For the rest of his life his old country described him contemptuously as being "unloyal." His story has given me much food for thought—he who for years was destined to embody disloyalty, was no more than a disorientated, directionless young man who couldn't cope with the repercussions of this confused identity. It's hard not to feel an enormous sympathy for that loquacious drunkard who at night, at least, could shout out desperately to the world that he couldn't carry on with the game. And so, curiously, among so many loyal individuals, the disloyal one was he who was too weak to play his part to the very end. The world wants this of us: that we keep to the script, that we carry on playing our role, that we stick to the character we've been asked to play. Loyalty means spending our lives in this theater, never moving away from the part we are playing, not even if the whiskey clouds our mind, leading us to shout out who we are and who we are not. And if we do, we become labeled by everyone as "unloyal," someone to be cursed. Freud wrote that when the city is quiet, during the hours of silence, only then do we allow ourselves to admit who we are. It is the key—magnificent and painful—that explains our dreams, and precisely because of their consummate truth, it constrains us to a coded language. A code, certainly. Of the kind used by spies.

Unloyalism—*noun.* Derived from the description of Donald Duart Maclean (1913–1983). *Indicates the state of mind of one in despair who no longer knows who he is, torn between what he would like to be and what he ought to be.*

Antonym:

Nellitude—*noun.* Derived from Nellie Bly (1864–1922). *Denotes the agility of one who succeeds in playing with a double identity, to obtain whatever advantage from it. Or simply to investigate the rock-hard identities of others.*

Villanism
or Vecellism

IT IS NO SMALL MYSTERY WHO BATTISTA DE VILLANIS really was. Starting even from the matter of gender: some historians claim he was a loyal servant, one of those who kept his master's most intimate secrets; others argue she was a woman, a tireless queen of the kitchen. What is certain is that Battista, in both cases, served the great Leonardo da Vinci, and when he died, in 1519, he or she received a substantial inheritance. Something unusual for an ordinary, perhaps illiterate, person to be so honored by one of Europe's most brilliant minds. Some versions, in truth, suggest that Leonardo had divided part of his possessions between his trusty servant Villanis and his cook Maturina. I cannot claim to be an expert on the interpretation of wills, but it suits my story to merge the two figures into one, that of the cook. So why should Leonardo, on his deathbed, want to remember a servant? This is the reason why our dictionary has chosen to coin a word dedicated to Battista de Villanis. As we shall see, the great Tuscan master seemed to have felt a need to take refuge in his very own real world, permeated with smells and offal, light-years away from the supposed Platonic realm of artists. Yes, you have to accept the evidence: there's plenty of it to show that Leonardo da Vinci had a genuine obsession with cooking, in pursuit of which he spent endless hours of his precious life sporting the proverbial sauce-splattered apron. Not surprisingly it's an aspect of his personality that the history books entirely ignore, almost as if it were shameful to admit that an intellectual of such caliber should waste time and energy on such demeaning activities.

Similarly, before embarking on a gastro-culinary account of Leonardo's life, let us step forward a few years in time to Pieve di Cadore in the Italian Veneto region and knock on the illustrious door of the Vecellio family, home of the famous painter Titian. Imagine the pride with which his family could boast that the branches of their tree included such a sublime artist, now the permanent official painter of the *Serenissima*. The fact remains that during the very same years Titian was at his peak, another Vecellio was born, almost in the same house, a young cousin, baptized with the name Cesare. And it was a tough life for the young boy, always in the shadow of his colossal relative, who had grown so famous that he was honored by Emperor Charles V of Habsburg with the titles of Count of the Lateran Palace, of the Aulic Council, and of the Consistory, Count Palatine, and Knight

of the Golden Spur. Like having a Nobel laureate in the house. He was unrivaled in wealth and honors. All the same, young Cesare also showed early promise as a painter, and tried in his own way to put it to good use. Around the mid-1500s he frescoed many churches and palaces in the Veneto region, suffering the embarrassment, goodness knows how many times, of having to explain that although his name was Vecellio, he wasn't *that* Vecellio but his cousin. For sure, friction between relatives is nothing new: just think, Karl Marx had a capitalist cousin who was a founder of Philips, which goes to show that long faces over Christmas lunch are not the sole prerogative of poor mortals. But this isn't why I have introduced that fine Vecellio junior. The point is that we are talking about him now, five centuries later, because he had a passion that was, in theory, far inferior and less lauded than painting, to be kept well hidden like Leonardo's enthusiasm for cooking.

Cesare Vecellio had a fixation with clothing.

If fashion magazines had existed at that time, he'd have subscribed to every one of them in order to follow the latest styles. There was no garment whose sartorial secrets he couldn't figure out in an instant, nor would a single detail escape him in headgear or footwear. All of this, of course, Cesare transformed into feverish graphic activity. He drew models dressed to the nines, involving him in frantic research into the latest fashions, so that it was rumored he was much in demand by noblewomen and dandies for expert advice on matters of beauty. In short, he soon became a prodigious sixteenth-century fashion blogger, and who knows what he might have done if the Vecellio household had had fewer tapestries and some semblance of an internet connection. For his part, Cesare compensated for it with decidedly international tastes—his figure drawings were infused with unusual exotic touches through exhaustive research into textiles and costumes from deepest Africa, from the Ottoman Empire as well as from the New World, even though Columbus's caravels had landed there less than a century before.

Fine, but how could our pioneer share his fine expertise with the human race and avoid compromising the glorious name of the other more famous Vecellio? It was no small matter. We can hardly bear to imagine Titian's fury when at high-society banquets he might have heard the request "Excuse me, Maestro, my wife has said I should ask your advice on whether to raise or lower the hem . . . " or "I saw your *Martyrdom of Saint Lawrence*, but why have you painted the figures half naked? I always follow your tips on matters of dress—do please clothe them all next time to give us a few ideas." This time it would have been for him to explain he wasn't *that* Vecellio but his cousin.

Then, in 1576, Titian was carried away by the plague, and it began a new chapter for Cesare. At last he could act freely, and he published what is to all intents and purposes the first modern treatise on fashion. You've heard of *Vogue*? Well, its prototype bore the name Vecellio. *Of Ancient and Modern Dress of Diverse Parts of the World* offers a unique outline of prehistoric prêt-à-porter, providing every kind of advice on what to wear and how to wear it, for special occasions and in everyday life. All, of course, carefully illustrated down to the smallest detail. It was enormously successful at the time, so that it was followed by at least two further editions, sufficient to confirm Cesare Vecellio as the highest authority on the subject, the tacit creator of a fall-winter and spring-summer collection that would set the standard for years to come.

And it mattered little if the clergy at Belluno Cathedral found themselves explaining that their *Saint Sebastian* (magnificent, all the same) was a youthful painting by a future Versace.

Well then, Leonardo da Vinci was fired by much the same passion, with the difference that he wouldn't pass into history for having written a recipe book. But let's rewind the tape.

It all began when his mother was married for the second time to a confectioner in Vinci, and Leonardo discovered that his stepfather was an undisputed genius with marzipan. During the ten years he lived with them, the boy watched and learned every secret about cakes and creams, spending his childhood in a kind of Hansel and Gretel biscuit world. Those were crucial years, which, as we know, leave their mark. And for him they certainly did. When his real father—Messer Piero, a notary—sent for him to study in Florence, a plump, chubby-cheeked little boy arrived at his house and spent almost the whole time, from morning to evening, talking about pastry and sultana pies. Lord help us. Fortunately, he was extremely good at drawing. For this, the little Botero was admitted to the workshop of Andrea del Verrocchio, Florence's leading authority on painting and sculpture, but also on mechanics. In short, it seemed that all was moving in the right direction, with some prospect that he might even lose weight.

Easily said.

For Leo's agreeable childhood was not so quickly forgotten, especially since the confectioner stepfather continued sending him every kind of iced tidbit from Vinci. Verrocchio was furious, tired of sweeping up bucketfuls of crumbs from under the easels, and he complained to the boy's father, the austere notary. All risked going badly wrong, and Leonardo was at a dramatic crossroads: he was about to finish up as the scullery boy to an elderly confectioner in Vinci, and we'd hear no more of him again. But no, instead it ended differently. The sources tell us repeatedly that the chubby adolescent was often punished for his guzzling, but what saved him was his unquestionable talent as an artist. And he proved it by painting one of the angels in Verrocchio's own *The Baptism of Christ*. Faced with the angel it was hard not to be amazed: the maestro and the notary looked at each other and agreed he had to continue, icing or no icing. In short, the boy may have been an unreformed fatty, but with a paintbrush he could produce miracles. Forget the cooking spoons.

His place as apprentice was given the thumbs-up.

For his part, the pupil set only one condition: that they would let him work each evening as a waiter at a certain Taverna delle Tre Lumache in the heart of Florence. And his request was granted, though later they would bitterly regret it when three cooks at the tavern were put out of action by unexplained poisoning, giving Leonardo a free hand to promote himself from waiter to chef . . .

Alas, a complete disaster.

Not just because the twenty-year-old took it into his head to quit Verrocchio's workshop—infuriating all those who believed in his genius as an artist—but above all because the Tre Lumache was a fairly simple establishment, known more than anything for a tasty polenta with meat sauce, which Leonardo took off the menu and replaced with culinary delicacies, daring accompaniments, and matching colors. After barely a month the customers rebelled: the Artusi from Vinci was pursued through the streets by a shower of pots and pans, from which he sought shelter in Verrocchio's arms.

We seem to see him pleading desperately, in tears: "Maestro, please can I come back?"

And the answer was yes, provided there was no more talk of cooking, not even inadvertently, not even metaphorically, not even indirectly.

Leonardo agreed, and carried on painting.

For several years it really seemed he had been cured. He no longer pontificated about cooking times and assorted garnishes, devoting himself instead to human anatomy and the study of perspective. He even lost weight. Verrocchio watched over him with his characteristic frown but was so proud to see him flourish under his wing, and in 1478 was delighted to give him his big chance—to paint an altarpiece for the chapel in Palazzo Vecchio. It would be the first real opportunity to demonstrate his true worth as an artist. "Are you pleased, Leonardo? You're worth this and more."

"You make me very happy, Maestro. Thank you, thank you."

And they embraced, as they had never done before. Oh, what a fine moment. But what a shame that another opportunity cropped up at that same time. The Taverna delle Tre Lumache went up in flames—Leonardo could take over its customers and open another tavern, avoiding the same errors as before. It was the lure of the kitchen. He recognized it immediately, as if he were being called back to his true mission. How could he resist? Cooking was his affliction and his passion, so he left Verrocchio, taking with him another pupil, Sandro Botticelli, another apostle of the divine Saucepan. To save money, they painted the new sign themselves (and weren't at all bad at it), SANDRO AND LEONARDO AT LE TRE RANE, and prepared a menu of dishes that were first-rate. Or so they reckoned. In good faith, for sure: they really believed in it.

To no avail. Once again it went wrong.

I don't know whether the food was as inedible as contemporary reports suggest. Maybe Florentine tastes were not yet ready. The fact remains that when the customers found four strips of carrot and an anchovy placed in a semicircle on the plate, they didn't care whether the arrangement was perfectly symmetrical and equidistant from the circumference of the plate—they sent it back. And the same for every other creative touch.

Sandro and Leonardo closed Le Tre Rane after a couple of weeks, amassing a heap of debts and so much local hatred that they even ran the risk of being lynched if they were seen together in the street: "It's those two from the tavern. Get a stick. I'll call in reinforcements. They need a good thrashing, otherwise they'll reopen."

And now the trouble really began. For this time they didn't even dare to knock on Verrocchio's door, and as for Lorenzo the Magnificent, it seemed the city's ruler wasn't so keen on the marzipan cakes Leonardo had sent him in the vain hope of his support. Only in 1482, when he was thirty, did one door open to recognize his genius: this was when Leonardo attended the court of Ludovico Sforza, duke of Milan, and handed him a letter of presentation. It was, I would say, a momentous letter—Leonardo described himself as excellent in painting and sculpture, boasted extraordinary abilities as a civil and military engineer, emphasizing at the end how "his cakes are unequalled."

And Ludovico hired him.

He would be in charge of military construction and at the same time would oversee the complex business of banquets, thus directing his beloved kitchens. For Leonardo it was pure bliss: he applied himself to both offices with such enthusiasm that he could even combine business with pleasure by presenting the duke with model fortifications made from marzipan and icing sugar. After which, of course, he spent a few days painting, but most of his energy went into the mad attempt to introduce machinery amid spit roasting and soup tureens. The *Codex Romanoff* offers us an incredible survey of Leonardo's projects specially designed for the Sforza kitchens in Milan. They range from a pedal-driven dryer (to move it required six sturdy men, taken from other duties), an automatic spit, an extractor fan, a wind-operated bread slicer, and an automatic beef mincer (into which the animal was introduced alive and kicking).

At first, Duke Ludovico encouraged the young man's enthusiasm, but he soon realized the phenomenon was growing to a worrying degree. Leonardo now saw the Sforza palace as an extension of the kitchen, which had been enlarged out of all proportion, and he went so far as to ask the elderly dowager duchess to vacate her apartments for the creation of a butchery and a fruit and vegetable store.

The matter was clearly getting out of hand, as was soon confirmed. When Leonardo appeared radiantly before Ludovico to announce he had completed a state-of-the-art kitchen for him, the duke decided to inaugurate it by holding a great banquet for lords, ladies, and cardinals. It was his way of bringing an end to the gradual expansion of the servants' area, which was now a sinister conglomeration of every kind of machinery, all bellows and blades. Leonardo for his part enthusiastically agreed, guaranteeing the success of the event. He didn't feel it necessary to tell the duke about the complaints he had received from the waiters, kitchen boys, and scullery maids. The atmosphere in the kitchen was infernal; the fearsome machinery absorbed all the workers' energy, slowing the cooking and compromising their safety. With an excess of caution, it seems, some of the cooks insisted on working in suits of armor so as not to end up being sliced like a ham, while the cleaners had to deal with a colossal machine for washing the floors, a kind of plow with cloths and rags that Leonardo had harnessed to two oxen.

It is not clear exactly what went wrong.

All we know is that in the middle of the banquet the guests heard terrible noises coming from the kitchen—piercing human cries, the yelping of miscellaneous animals, explosions, smashed dishes, an indescribable pandemonium of imprecations and abuse. The situation was deteriorating fast, so that Leonardo himself, half injured and burned, had to appear before the guests to announce that, due to unexpected technical difficulties, the dishes on the menu would be replaced with a salad.

Next day the casualties were counted.

Leonardo's kitchen machinery may have been ingenious, but it had brought catastrophe on a par with the bloodiest battles. Not surprisingly it was decided to redesignate the mighty automatic meat mincer with revolving blades for use as a war machine, which proved indeed to be a terrifying spectacle.

In other words, he tried as best as he could to put a positive spin on the day.

But it wasn't easy. How could it be, for heaven's sake, with matrons leaving the banquet in shock, the stoves dripping with blood, and storerooms full of dead bodies?

Duke Ludovico was furious, to say the least. He imposed a strict ban on Leonardo entering the kitchens and placed armed guards at the doors. From then on, he would be allowed only to paint, better still if he kept a long way from the palace.

Leonardo came close to losing his nerves, and his sleep. Then he had a brilliant idea. His work of art would be a banquet, a *Last Supper*, to be painted in the convent refectory at Santa Maria delle Grazie. The duke was obviously delighted and gave instructions for the great artist to be lodged with the friars. How could he imagine that even there he would stir a culinary panic? How could he imagine that the eel and the turnip purée painted on the table before the disciples would be the cause for more pandemonium in the convent kitchens? On the occasion of Easter 1496, the prior of Santa Maria delle Grazie wrote a sad letter to the duke: Leonardo da Vinci may well be a very great painter, but the friars are dying of hunger. It marked the beginning of a war that would end only with the last brushstroke of the masterpiece. There, in effect, Leonardo brought together his two consuming passions, painting and cooking. It would be impossible to consider one aspect without the other: he put the two together, regarding himself as a painter and a cook at the same time. And even in the years to come, he was unable or unwilling to ignore either of them. So that, like it or not, the complete picture of Leonardo is one of a man who arrived in France in 1516, to the court of King Francis. With him was his beloved Battista de Villanis (she who had helped him years before in the kitchen) and then—his only baggage—a canvas and a rectangular box of a disturbingly dark color. They were his inseparable masterpieces: the *Mona Lisa* and the machine he had devised to turn sheets of pasta into edible strings.

Yes, Leonardo invented spaghetti too.

Villanism; also, Vecellism—*nouns*. Derived from the cook Battista de Villanis (fifteenth to sixteenth century) and from Cesare Vecellio (1521–1601). *Describes the marvelous energy that leads you to doggedly pursue your natural vocation. Whether the others like it or not, you cannot but follow it, for it is part of you.*

Z

Zacharian _and_ Zeissian

WHEN WE SEE, WHAT DO WE REALLY SEE? There was a time, long ago, when our eyes determined everything. It seems impossible today, but for thousands of years human beings had to rely on their sight alone, however defective and limited. There were no ways of correcting short- or long-sightedness, of identifying colorblindness: it made no difference whether vision was blurred or the colors distorted; everything was part of the great world spectacle. Seeing things was experiencing reality, and the eyes, guardians of our senses, were guarantors of objectivity, taking a leading, almost tyrannical role against such prime adversaries as the mouth and nose (for breathing) and the ears (for hearing). Everything started and ended with seeing, and this is why there's a proliferation of words to express this supreme optical power, from *visual* to *vision*, from *foresee* to *envisage*. In short, the eyes are said to give us the correct idea about things without distorting them. And yet today we take it so for granted that our technology can alter proportions, enlarging or reducing them as required, with the result that the ancient—or, if you like, biological—experience of seeing has now become the baseline of a continual zoom. Didn't Pliny write that the emperor Nero used a kind of emerald to improvise the effect of binoculars at gladiatorial games? Well, that was just the beginning. It grew from there, and now our eyes are no longer enough. As instruments, we regard them as limited, demeaning, subject to glaucoma and cataracts, always—inevitably—requiring assistance to obtain an all-round visual experience. In short, we are no longer content to accept sight as a simple physiological act, but instead we expect to take control of the view, just like in a video recording studio. With the tips of two fingers we enlarge or reduce the pictures on our smartphones—a small-scale reproduction, in effect, of what humanity has done for centuries with telescopes and microscopes.

This is what we will be talking about in the last part of our dictionary: about big things, small things, and about our incapacity to see them as such, accustomed as we are to changing their size according to the needs of the moment. It all began with binoculars. Or rather, with a bitter struggle over the patent. Rarely had an invention caused such a stir. It happened about a year before the day in August 1609 when Galileo climbed Saint Mark's Campanile in Venice to show his astronomic telescope to the city governors. It is well known that Galileo's essential contribution was to devise a scientific use for something that had in fact been

developed not by him but by some Dutch lens grinders, people who were considered social outcasts because they followed a profession that, in effect, distorted the actual outlines of objects. It may come as a harsh disappointment for some—I don't know—but resign yourselves to the fact that Galileo didn't invent the telescope: he almost certainly had one delivered from the Dutch city of Middelburg several months before presenting his version for astronomical purposes in Venice. I think it's worth looking more closely, then, at the story of this group of Dutch lens grinders, not least because it well illustrates what we were saying about the distortion of reality.

In 1600, Hans Lippershey was just over thirty, a man with the open, innocent gaze of a child yet, as a grown-up, still taken by surprise at each of life's storms. One might almost say that he wasn't living but was playing at living, assembling the pieces with the unconscious delight a three-year-old displays while pretending to set water on fire. Well, Lippershey practiced his dubious business of lens grinding with the same lightness, a craft little tolerated by the authorities of Middelburg. We'll find this more understandable when we remember that Galileo, around that same time, was almost reported to the Holy Inquisition for being paid sixty lire in exchange for astrological horoscopes. He was apparently very good (a real champion who would have drawn excellent ratings on Sunday night TV with a title such as *Galileo Reads Our Stars*), but I wouldn't say it was a very prestigious move for a scientist at Padua University. And you can imagine how the Inquisition might have reacted. In Protestant Holland in the early 1600s, on the other hand, there was no religious condemnation of spectacle-makers, even though they moved in a secret, murky, almost necromantic underworld. Their craft had nothing to do with medicine but was perceived, if anything, as a kind of oddball phenomenon, to such an extent that even today the word *spectacles* has a double meaning: *entertainments* but also *glasses*. And it was this kind of circus showmanship that Lippershey, one fine morning, thought of using to surprise a group of children who were sitting in the street outside the humble house in which he lived and worked. In fact, there are those who suggest that his interest in showmanship was altogether secondary and that Lippershey was trying in vain to make ends meet during a lean month. Be that as it may, thin as a rake, with a face like a dried prune, he went out into the street whistling, stopped a few feet away from the bunch of kids busily playing marbles, and casually threw out a challenge: "You see that weather vane up there, that metal rooster that turns in the wind? I'll pay half a florin to anyone who can tell me how many points there are to the comb on its head."

With their marbles still in their hands, they turned their dirty snouts toward him, looking him up and down as if he were crazy (which didn't surprise them at all, since Lippershey made diabolical instruments to change the colors and lines of everything).

"Ain't possible. Too far away to see!" muttered the toughest of the ten, son of the smartest blacksmith in Middelburg. He hadn't realized that this was exactly the answer Lippershey was hoping for: "Correct! So you pay me two florins—you to me—if I can make you see that faraway rooster close up."

At this point the urchins put their marbles in their pockets. It seemed much more profitable to check out the stupidity of the spectacle-maker. "And what do we make out of it?" asked the same one, the leader.

"You'll make ten florins, which I'll pay—one to each of you—if the rooster isn't close enough for you to count the number of points on its comb." And he smiled, trying to look like a village idiot so they'd agree to the bet. Which indeed they did.

"Deal done, Master Lippershey, but I have to see the rooster right here, a foot away," added the blacksmith's son.

"Even closer: I'll bring it right before your eyes, not even a palm's width from your nose!" shouted the spectacle-maker as he went off to his cupboard to retrieve a wooden tube with some lenses inside, remnants from goodness knows what contraption. They were the toys that Lippershey happened to make, between one job and another, amusing himself by mounting lenses inside them for no particular purpose. If you like, we might say he was fooling his own eyes, constantly muddling the spectacle of reality. Except that on this day, for the first time, without even realizing it, Lippershey was about to share one of his toys with the rest of the world . . .

Goodness! That's impossible.

The rooster had three points on its comb, the middle one being taller and rusty, giving it almost a red touch of pictorial realism. For the children, of course, it was more of a disappointment than a miraculous discovery. They passed the infernal contraption between them, not so much to admire the rooster but for final confirmation that they had frittered away their two florins. As for the blacksmith's son, it goes without saying that he handed over the money but made the gang pay for it.

Yet what the spectacle-maker never expected that day was the reaction of passersby, a growing crowd of ordinary folk, drawn at first by curiosity . . . Then more and more of them asked to share the most thrilling experience of the century, to turn a miniature rooster into a colossal feathered monument.

Isn't this, after all, what is continually going on in our minds? We are magnifying everything, transforming insignificant details into major issues; we attach terrible importance to circumstantial and hypothetical situations, continually distorting the actual substance of things. We live in fear, and fear is nothing more than the tiny faraway rooster multiplied in size until it seems to loom right over us. In that dusty street in Middelburg, however, Master Lippershey had just succeeded in bringing this curse out from within us, giving the mechanism real concrete form.

What an extraordinary discovery!

That's right, so extraordinary that when Lippershey hurried to register the patent in 1608 with the name *optic tube*, he had no idea it would be a hard battle. For it just so happened that another inventor was about to turn up with the same discovery, a certain irascible Jacob Metius, quarrelsome like few others, and convinced that his own claim was beyond dispute. As soon as he discovered there was some debate over it, Metius flew into a rage, and though well aware that he had registered the patent three weeks after Lippershey's, he had it recorded that his warehouse was full of the most brilliant inventions the likes of which would amaze the whole ungrateful human world: in the event of his death, they had to set fire to everything to prevent others claiming paternity. This gives some idea of the tone of the argument, in what was in all respects the War of the Three Patents. Yes, three. Because poor Lippershey also had to deal with a third rival, far wilder than Metius. Along the same street—just a few doors from where he lived—was a sinister figure known to everyone as Zacharias, one who had always survived on his wits, if not actually dishonestly. Zacharias came from the south of Holland and had been highly ambitious from a young age. Always going one better, at whatever cost. His father had moved from town to town as an itinerant peddler, but Zacharias wanted to do better, to reach the top, to redouble his profits, and to do so he tried out every kind of deceit, from miraculous ointments to potions against gout. But he didn't stop there: bored of this fairground gimcrackery, he soon opted for more lucrative activities, including a clandestine mint, for which he was investigated several times and convicted of forgery. You may ask: how could a character like that end up playing a part in the glorious history of telescopes? As I say, Zacharias lived very close to Master Lippershey, and several years after the story of the rooster, two young sons of a certain Lowyssen—a lens grinder too—were placed in his care. It's a detail of no secondary importance that, along with the children, Zacharias came into possession of the deceased spectacle-maker's entire workshop. Thousands of lenses. What could he do with them? Would someone like him ever stoop to making spectacles? No indeed. Zacharias was never content—greatness was his obsession—so he immediately realized that the real masterstroke would be to make binoculars, the innovation of the century patented by his neighbor. After all, his motto throughout life had been: Make small things seem enormous. Rooster combs were kids' stuff. So Zacharias turned up at the patent office too, not merely claiming paternity of the invention but presenting in his favor a whole array of witnesses—people of dubious background, undoubtedly well paid—ready to declare that Master Lippershey had entered Zacharias's workshop one night and stolen his invention. An investigation began: which of the two was lying?

The dispute went on for years. It didn't end until halfway through the century with the victory of Zacharias's son, who had inherited his methods: he even went as far as falsifying dates of birth in order to justify his own position. In the meantime, both Lippershey and Zacharias had died, as well as the cantankerous Jacob Metius (and with him all his mysterious contraptions, set on fire by the disposition in his will). We should add that meanwhile, in Venice, Signor Galileo had obtained an appointment for life (at double salary) when he presented an improved version of the telescope as his own exclusive invention.

There was no way out: the Dutch authorities were forced to recognize what to everyone seemed intolerable, namely that the crooked Zacharias—who knew as much about lenses as Julius Caesar did about computers—had invented the modern telescope. It was a blatant distortion of reality, which is even more striking if we think what was written on the patent: the technical use of concave and convex lenses to make what is distant seem close. A breathtaking optical deceit was accompanied by a scurrilous moral deceit, the transformation of a petty swindler into a wondrous genius. In short, a question of apparent (false) dimensions. But a question of apparent (false) dimensions was, in the end, the basis for the whole of our modern era, which was timidly emerging at that very moment. And perhaps I'm not the only one to think this story tells us something about our obsession with always having to go further, constantly aiming for the best, the top, the record: this was how Zacharias saw it (and he ended up as the victor).

But if, in conclusion, we try a different path?

Carl Zeiss, for example, is rather the opposite of Zacharias. We are now in Germany in the early 1800s—two centuries have passed since the Dutch patent war, and telescopes are now scanning the sky far and wide in search of nebulae, comets, galaxies, and asteroids. In Weimar, a child is born, the son of a toymaker. I have always been struck by this detail about Zeiss: he grew up—with many brothers and sisters—in a world of wooden trains, dolls, spinning tops, lead soldiers, tin cottages, puppets, marionettes, and so on and so forth—all those playfellows from that time in life when everything has to fit in the palm of your hand. This is the essential rule about toys: they reduce the dimensions of true reality, narrowing and decreasing the risks so that the child has full control—no adult could ever hold an entire railroad convoy in the palm of his hand, but his young child can, in the same way that she can hold to her breast a tiny reproduction of a princess in costume. Isn't this a distortion too? Yes, of course: a close encounter with a grizzly bear in a forest can be fatal for a human being, and yet a child won't go to sleep without his teddy bear. And so these were the very objects that Carl Zeiss's father was making in Germany in 1820: cozy miniatures of reality, devised to give the illusion that everything outside can be known in advance, on a smaller scale. Maybe this is why the old games have gone out of fashion today: we immediately want to aim big, with no gradual increase, with no in-between, convinced as we are that timely weaning is the only weapon in the jungle that awaits us. Well, in all of this, the case of Carl Zeiss teaches us quite the opposite: son of a toymaker, he never lost his passion for small things, for hidden secrets, for treasures to be found in boxes and the solution of a puzzle. Before he was thirty he was clear about his future: he would produce microscopes. He wouldn't look up toward the immense distances of the stars measured at the speed of light; no, he would turn his gaze to infinite smallness, to the microcosm of matter, where organic processes lay concealed. And so while the telescope tried to satisfy our need to understand what we have above us, Zeiss's microscopes examined the opposite problem: what we have inside.

Who knows—perhaps this is why I feel a deep sympathy for this toymaker's son who was never tempted by any concern about world systems, about the unfathomable, about the enormity of space. He devoted all his energy to the study of the smallest dimensions while everyone was stargazing, and he turned it into a legendary trademark. So that, ironically, Zeiss's greatness was due to his passion for something infinitely small. Our whole existence, as we know, is woven from a multitude of observation points.

But each observation is—always—the story of a choice.

Zacharian—*adjective*. Derived from Zacharias Janssen (1585–c. 1632). *Describes the frantic attitude of someone who is prepared to pay whatever price in order to aim big.*

Antonym:

Zeissian—*adjective*. Derived from the optical instrument maker Carl Zeiss (1816–1888). *Denotes the choice of one who is prepared not necessarily to aim big but prefers to examine the problem of what is contained in the smallest objects.*

About the Author

Stefano Massini is an internationally renowned novelist, essayist, and playwright. His plays, including his celebrated *The Lehman Trilogy*, have been translated into twenty-seven languages and staged by such directors as Luca Ronconi and Oscar-winning Sam Mendes. *Qualcosa sui Lehman* has been among the most acclaimed novels published in Italy in recent years and won the Premio Selezione Campiello, the Premio Super Mondello, the Premio De Sica, the Prix Médicis Essai, and the Prix du Meilleur Livre Étranger. His other works include *Ladies Football Club*.

A Note from the Translator

A good translation should make readers feel the author is speaking directly to them rather than talking over a cultural fence. My task is to remove such a barrier and try to place English-speaking readers, as far as possible, in the same position as those of the original text.

A historical reference, for example, might be clear to an Italian reader though obscure to a foreigner. Any Italian will know about Lorenzo the Magnificent without having to be told that he ruled Florence in the late-fifteenth century, but an English reader may be lost without an extra word or two of explanation. Other references may be so unfathomable that it would require a whole history lesson to explain them. A passing reference to an Italian battle in Ethiopia or a geographical detail introduced merely for color might be better replaced by alternatives that produce a similar effect so that little is lost.

What, on the other hand, will the English reader make of the story about Leonardo da Vinci who, when his culinary prowess was put to the test, is described as the "Artusi from Vinci"? Every Italian reader would recognize the allusion to the august cookery writer Pellegrino Artusi, Italy's equivalent of Mrs. Beaton. Here I have kept the original reference, recognizing that many Anglophone readers will have to work a little harder to understand, but knowing that the internet is always there to help.

The translation must seek to replicate the author's own distinctive voice. Massini is a natural storyteller and uses every oral device to hold his audience's attention. I have tried to preserve the color and cadences of his dialogue so that it flows as naturally as the original text.

The author uses historical characters and events to construct stories in which there is no clear boundary between historical fact and fiction. He uses the conventions of cinema and theater to give his characters lines they probably never spoke and to make them perform deeds about which history is silent. Their exploits are wound into an intriguing series of meditations on aspects of human nature for which no dictionary has yet found a word . . . until now.

—Richard Dixon

Here ends Stefano Massini's
The Book of Nonexistent Words.

The first edition of this book was printed
and bound at Worzalla Publishing,
Stevens Point, Wisconsin, in September 2021.

A NOTE ON THE TYPE

The text of this novel was set in Adobe Garamond, a typeface designed in 1989 by Robert Slimbach. It was based on
two distinctive examples of the French Renaissance style: a
roman type by Claude Garamond (1499–1561) and an italic
type by Robert Granjon (1513–1590). The typeface was developed after Slimbach studied the fifteenth-century equipment
at the Plantin-Moretus Museum in Antwerp, Belgium. Adobe
Garamond faithfully captures the original Garamond's grace
and clarity, and it is used extensively in print for its elegance
and readability.

HarperVia

An imprint dedicated to publishing international voices,
offering readers a chance to encounter other lives and other
points of view via the language of the imagination.